ROGUES:

Alpha Male Short Story Collection

Edited by Delilah Devlin

Swindled Copyright © 2016 Megan Mitcham
Opals Copyright © 2016 Axa Lee
Her Heart's Tomb Copyright © 2016 Jennifer Kacey
The Highwayman's Treasure Copyright © 2016 Emma Jay
Plunder Copyright © 2016 Delilah Night
The Heat Copyright © 2016 Mia Hopkins
The Highwayman Came Riding Copyright © 2016 Erzabet Bishop
Queen High Copyright © 2016 Cela Winter
Rogue Hearts Copyright © 2016 Delilah Devlin
Lady of the House Copyright © 2016 T.G. Haynes
Billionaire and the Jewel Thief Copyright © 2016 Elle James
An Eye for Love Copyright © 2016 Cynthia Young
Roguishly Handsome, and Other Superhero Problems Copyright © 2016 Tray Ellis
Glass Slippers, Hardly Worn Copyright © 2016 Bibi Rizer

Print Edition

Last-round edits by **LustreEditing.com**,
a full-service freelance fiction editing company

The stories in this book are works of fiction. The characters, incidents, and dialogues are of the authors' imaginations and are not to be construed as real. Any resemblance to actual events or persons, living or dead, is completely coincidental.

ALL RIGHTS RESERVED. This book is licensed for your personal enjoyment only. No part of this book may be reproduced or transmitted in any form or by any means, electronic or mechanical, including photocopying, recording, or by an information storage and retrieval system without permission in writing from the authors—except by a reviewer who may quote brief passages in a review to be printed in a magazine, newspaper, or on the web.

This book may not be re-sold or given away to other people. If you would like to share this book with another person, please purchase an additional copy for each recipient. If you're reading this book and did not purchase it, purchase your own copy. Thank you for respecting the hard work of these authors.

Rogues! Even the word conjures a special sort of hero—a playful bad boy with a heart of gold—at least when it comes to his lady love.

This volume is filled with the Jack Sparrows of old—pirates sailing the high seas, Regency-era highway men, modern day jewel thieves, like Cary Grant in *To Catch a Thief*—men doing bad things, bending or breaking the law, but in a very sexy way.

With fourteen stories sure to satisfy the reader who craves that ultimate bad boy, prepare to have your heart stolen!

Contents

Introduction	vii
SWINDLED – Megan Mitcham	1
OPALS – Axa Lee	21
HER HEART'S TOMB – Jennifer Kacey	34
THE HIGHWAYMAN'S TREASURE – Emma Jay	54
PLUNDER – Delilah Night	74
THE HEAT – Mia Hopkins	96
THE HIGHWAYMAN CAME RIDING – Erzabet Bishop	114
QUEEN HIGH – Cela Winter	125
ROGUE HEARTS – Delilah Devlin	146
LADY OF THE HOUSE – T. G. Haynes	165
BILLIONAIRE & THE JEWEL THIEF – Elle James	181
AN EYE FOR LOVE – Cynthia Young	203
ROGUISHLY HANDSOME, AND OTHER SUPERHERO PROBLEMS – Tray Ellis	223
GLASS SLIPPERS, HARDLY WORN – Bibi Rizer	241
About the Authors	259
About The Editor	263

Introduction

Rogues! Even the word conjures a special sort of hero—a playful bad boy with a heart of gold—at least when it comes to his lady love.

This volume is filled with the Jack Sparrows of old—pirates sailing the high seas, Regency-era highway men, modern day jewel thieves, like Cary Grant in *To Catch a Thief*—men doing bad things, bending or breaking the law, but in a very sexy way.

With fourteen stories sure to satisfy the reader who craves that ultimate bad boy, prepare to have your heart stolen!

I'll admit it. I love my job. I get to read authors' submissions then choose those I love the most. Sometimes, it's excruciating narrowing the field when there are more stories that I love than I can include. Such was the case with this collection. I hope you enjoy the result. All the stories showcase the authors' vivid imaginations. All portray familiar tropes you'll recognize and appreciate, but with twists. There's a variety of sexy situations and heat levels, but the common denominator is always the rogue—that man you know you shouldn't want but can't help falling for.

Happy reading!
Delilah Devlin

Swindled

Megan Mitcham

HARPER LANG SNAGGED a flute from the service waiter and cursed the vibrant white room. *Why the hell did art installations have to be so damn bright?* Thanks to long New York winters and blink-and-you'll-miss-them summers, her pasty complexion hadn't seen sun in the ten years she'd lived in the city. Nor had her face seen this much make-up. She probably looked like a street hooker working her way up to professional escort. Well, she was working. A smile tickled her lips while the bubbling champagne did the same to the back of her throat.

Yep, she was a naughty girl. Drinking on the job.

She downed the remainder of the sparkling wine in an unladylike gulp, set the glass on a planter that looked like it had contracted red and white polka-dotted measles, and strode toward the nearest excuse for art. Her public school upbringing didn't count the pile of day-glow vomit in the shape of an extra-large housefly as art.

Vincent. Claude. Michelangelo. Those were her guys.

Igmon Yeaveas, the featured artist of the night didn't hold a candle to their talents. *That* fraud didn't lure her here tonight, but for some incomprehensible reason, he attracted the Big Apple's nobility and their pocketbooks. And they in turn drew Baron Magnus Declan.

At least, Harper hoped they did. Otherwise, she'd wasted three hundred bucks on a half-priced cocktail dress and two hundred more on four-inch stilettos. Maybe, when she needed a pick-me-up, she'd wear the curve-hugging lace and spikes around her closet-sized apartment.

Her gut vibrated with excitement. After months of research and two near misses, this was the night she'd arrest the world-renowned swindler. She'd earn a stripe on her shiny new detective's shield and maybe get assigned one of the good cases. Missing persons, rape, homicide. The possibilities stiffened her nipples. Not the atrocities, but catching the real scum of the earth. Who cared about some Rico Suave talking rich broads into bed and out of their inherited dough?

Harper tugged the low-cut fabric toward the ceiling to conceal her peaked twins. The black material managed not to move an inch.

"Quit fidgeting," her partner's smoke-scarred voice cracked in her ear through a tiny comm link.

"How the hell are you inside? Is he here?" she whispered.

"Nah, still in the car. I swing my pot-belly in that place, and we'd lose Declan forever. I just know you, girly. Anytime you get dolled up, you wring your hands like a perp."

She smoothed a hand over her bosom and down the narrow curve of her hips. These double-D cups belonged on another woman's body. A stripper's, perhaps. They only brought lecherous attention and grief on the force. People thought big boobs equaled a small brain. Even women. So, yeah, she'd kept them on lock-down for so long she didn't know how to act with them on display. Yet, for the first time, Harper appreciated her chest. They'd landed her this gig. Russell had twenty-five years on the force but didn't possess the goods to ensnare the thief. She had the rack, half-a-million in borrowed diamonds, a rented limo, and a silver clutch worth more than the gun inside and the one strapped to her thigh combined.

"We'll get this guy, Lang. All we need is some damn proof."

Shoulders back. Chin up. Mouth pursed like the captain showed you. Interested, but not impressed. Boobs in. Think high society. Be upper crust.

By the time she lapped the room, the fizzy allayed her discomfort. The hot stares from two Wall Street suit types helped too. Harper's gaze roved the sea of sequins, feathers, tweed, and skin in search of her quarry.

"You see him yet?" Russell barked. "All I got are alley rats, a homeless guy, and wait staff."

"Nothing."

The glass door opened and closed frequently, bearing couture-labeled couples like the stadium turnstile produced Yankee fans. But no Declan.

★ ★ ★

THREE HOURS LATER, the crowd had thinned, her feet ached, and an edgy quality hugged her so tightly it cut off circulation to her brain. At eight years old, she'd read *A Study in Scarlett* and had wanted to be Sherlock Holmes ever since. She'd used logic and Declan's developed patterns from years of swindling women in Europe to formulate the perfect trap for the man. He hadn't even shown his face much less taken the bait. Feeling more like Addison Holmes than Sherlock, Harper closed her eyes, balled her fists, and willed him there.

"I'm callin' it, Lang."

"No, Russ. Give me ten more minutes," she begged.

"He's usually in some lady's bed by this time of night. Whether he pegged us from the door or didn't hunt these waters, we missed him."

"Five more minutes?" she negotiated.

"Girly, this job is rife with disappointment. Better get used to it now and invest in hair dye. Your black locks are gonna go gray before you know it. I mean, look at my hair." He chuckled at himself. "Oh, wait, I don't have any."

"Ha. Ha." She groaned.

"I'm outta here. Want a ride?"

She plucked two glasses of champagne from a passing server, took a step toward the backdoor and her partner, but stopped short. The department had already paid for the limo. It'd be a shame to waste it on account of a no-show. "I'll see you Monday, old man."

"Be safe. Some of these high-brow types are mean

bastards," Russell warned.

"I'm meaner."

"Sure are."

Harper chugged the contents of the first glass and left it in the care of another waiter. The suckers crawled through the place like worker ants. She pulled the transmitter from her ear, dropped the thing into her clutch, and snarled as it *clinked* on the gun and handcuffs. Seemed like none of them were getting any action tonight.

Disappointment cut deep. Spinning in a leisurely circle, she cataloged the remaining patrons, craving something to dull the edge of disappointment. The bubbly wouldn't work on her Italian and Japanese roots. They'd been saturated in sake and limoncello from a young age. Adding defeat to desperation, none of the fellas seemed fit for the job. Neither the barely pubescent servers nor the ego-inflated suits wagging their brows would do. Tonight, she needed a man to toss her onto, well, anywhere and make things happen.

Too bad her best chances of orgasm tonight came from Danny the Drawer Dick. Harper tipped back the other glass of wine, sipping this time. She savored the taste of liquid money and mentally shrugged.

At least Danny's reliable. Until there's a battery shortage.

As the bottom of her glass came into view, something brushed her upper lip. She righted the flute in a blink and braced for the bug or who-knew-what that surely sat at the bottom.

"What?" she hissed.

In the dregs of her champagne sat a big ass canary yellow diamond. Her gaze shot left and flew right in search of Declan. But no one paid her any attention. Not even the lanky waiter.

"Son of a bitch. He was here, and he knew we were, too."

She poured the remainder of the champagne into a planter and pinched the three-and-a-half carat rock between her thumb and index finger. The only thing she hated more than losing was being made to look like a fool. Magnus Declan had succeeded where most failed. She held one of three diamonds reported stolen by Declan's ex-wife, Baroness Genevieve DuMau, and bit back a curse.

MAGNUS PEERED THROUGH the one-way glass overlooking the dwindling crowd, but saw only Detective Harper Lang. The woman sucking his lobe faded deeper into the background. Wasn't it a dangerous thing when a woman could draw you in with a slant of her brow while an heiress couldn't faze you by offering a blow job?

Hell, yes!

But it wouldn't stop him. He'd been pursued by women since before his balls dropped. Yet, never quite like this. Harper had been on his heels for weeks, and all he wanted was hers tossed over his shoulders. Well, not all. He wanted to watch her face flush with ecstasy as he slid inside her. The thrill worked him over in ways he'd never known existed in his thirty-five years, and twenty of those had been lived on the edge of legal and off the cliff of moral.

The black-eyed, porcelain-faced beauty chunked the flute into the large planter, dropped the diamond into her purse, and stomped toward the hallway which led to the restrooms. A grin quirked his mouth.

"Let's go." He shrugged the woman off his ear and hauled her behind him down the stairs, through the corridor, and to the entrance of the women's bathroom. When he finally turned and looked down, her light blue eyes glittered mischievously. A little too much like his own. "You come, and then you go. You're not the one who'll change me or pin me down. You don't love me. You don't know me, and probably have no idea what love really is. Understand?" Her eager hand shot to his fly. "You. Not me."

"Okay," she panted, flashing blinding white caps and batting fake lashes.

So much in his world was fake, he longed for something real. This probably wasn't the best way to go about getting it, but it sure stirred his blood.

DETERMINED TO SEARCH the kitchen and back rooms before heading home, Harper flushed. The door opened and a giggle accompanied two sets of shoes. Reaching for her matching lace thong, she continued righting herself.

"But someone's in here," a woman whispered.

Harper hurried to smooth her dress and split before

the chick pulled out a bag of smack. There was only one person worth arresting tonight, and his voice was deeper than that.

"I know," rumbled the voice she'd swear her mind conjured.

She'd listened to that gooey caramel tone for hours on end. Following along with the translations hadn't diminished its panty-dropping effect. But that couldn't be Declan. Not after the stunt he'd pulled.

A throaty moan split the air. Harper flushed rooftop-in-July-hot and clamped a hand over her own mouth. She didn't want to get caught in the middle of a fuck-fest, unless she was center stage. If it was in fact Magnus Declan, she had to know. Yet, she couldn't risk chasing him away by barging out of the stall unprepared.

"Ooohhh, yes," the woman groaned, "right there."

Curse her body to hell and back. Harper's lady boner swelled to life as though it garnered the attention being awarded another. Releasing her mouth, she inhaled a deep quiet breath and steadied one hand on the metal wall. With the other, she grabbed her clutch from the top of the paper rack. One more fortifying breath and she leaned toward the two-inch gap between the door and stall.

Her heart ping-ponged between her belly and throat.

Baron Magnus Declan's hips nestled in the V of a woman's legs. Her blue dress fanned on the counter around her bare bottom while her panties dangled from the tip of a jeweled, white Manolo. Only the angle allowed the full view because his breadth could easily hide a slight woman or two. The broad's head arched toward the ceiling, missing the best part of the whole damn experience.

The man's face was the only thing in all of Manhattan worthy of being called art. His wide jaw looked like it could take a solid punch, while his lips could kiss any hurt away. And those azure blue eyes…

Oh god, he's looking right at me.

Thinking she may have been mistaken, Harper didn't move. She didn't want to draw his attention. But the longer she watched, the more clear it became. His fingers worked the woman splayed on the counter, but he stared into her eyes. The woman's hips rocked. His gaze did not.

An orange, spray-tanned hand coasted over his shoulder, and his gaze snapped away. "Grip the counter," he demanded.

Harper covered her heart with her hand, trying to stop the frantic rhythm. She only succeeded in stimulating her nipples. In a flash, his blue eyes returned to her. The attention seared hot in her core. He flicked the woman's clit and finger fucked her to the most intense orgasm Harper had ever experienced—and he hadn't even touched her. She hadn't even touched herself. Well, not much. Yet, her fingers bit into the clutch, her breath stalled, her body quaked. The lace of her bodice crushed under her grip. All the while, he watched her through the tiny slit. And she didn't dare blink.

Weak-kneed and close to tears when the woman straightened her dress, Harper stumbled backward and gripped the metal bar she'd never before dared to touch in any bathroom stall. Her heart stormed inside her chest, which was minimal in comparison to what her brain did. Guilt and confusion assaulted her for a long minute, but stubborn pride lifted her chin. Manolos *clacked* across the short room. Air shifted, and the door met the frame with a *thud*. Though she couldn't see him, she knew he remained.

The bastard.

Determination straightened her shoulders. She had done nothing wrong, though the wetness between her legs called her a liar.

Lusting wasn't illegal.

The water turned on at the sink. Harper exhaled and stepped out of the stall. Declan's knowing gaze held her own as she walked to the nearest sink. She turned the faucet on and lathered soap, nearly mimicking his movements.

"What kind of name is Magnus, anyway?" Harper asked.

The corner of his mouth quirked before thinning. He dried thick hands, tossed the cloth into a wicker hamper, and then snagged hers and did the same. His gaze considered her like she were an intricate puzzle. "The only thing my mother gave me before divorcing my father for a younger hotter version with less baggage, taking her money with her, and leaving me and my siblings destitute."

She hadn't expected that, but tried not to show it. Probably wasn't true anyway. Just something to sway her feminine emotions. "Am I supposed to feel sorry for you? Is that your excuse for using women like disposable rags?" She nodded toward the hamper.

"If you'd paid attention, and I think you did," his pink lips spread wide at that, "you'd recall mutual using going on. Women and men have been using each other for piles of centuries. It won't stop anytime soon."

"What does your wife think about that?"

"Ex-wife," he corrected, smoothing his dark blond brow.

Of all things, her pulse skittered at the stroke of his finger across the coarse hair. He rubbed a thumb over his lower lip, taunting her. "I wanted a title. She wanted security."

"Security?" Harper swallowed.

"In the bank account and bedroom." He stepped forward, brushing the lace of her dress with his high-end suit's buttons. His breath tickled her cheek as he leaned down. "Her extravagant lifestyle and first marriage left her in need. Do you know anything about need, Harper?"

"Detective Lang," she snapped. Or at least, she tried. His manly scent and proximity screwed with her senses. She breathed deeply, fighting to ignore the brush of her nipples against his chest. "Why did you give me the diamond?"

"Have it tested. It's not the piece from her family's collection, which she sold five years ago, but one I purchased to replace them on our three-year anniversary. It's a quarter carat larger."

Harper collected every speck of self-control she possessed, planted two hands on his chest, and shoved. The big man only moved an inch, but it was enough that she squeezed between him and the wall and hurried toward the door.

"Aren't you going to cuff me?"

She didn't have anything to hold him, but still she stopped with one hand on the door.

"No, you're not," he said, drawing nearer. "You don't want anyone to know I made you come without a single touch." Looming over her shoulder, the heat of his large body shot a wave of gooseflesh across hers. "I've never seen such an honest reaction in my life, and that's a treasure too exquisite to share."

DAMN! HE WAS good. No wonder women tossed themselves at him, along with anything else he wanted. Harper stomped her rage on each of the seventy-two stairs it took to reach her apartment door. She'd done many difficult things on the force, but none had come close to walking away from Magnus Declan. Pheromones wafted off the man's skin in potent waves as detrimental as forest fires. But the unexpected sincerity, combined with his uninhibited manner, proved the most dangerous aspect, aside from his pure physicality.

A single lamp welcomed Harper home. She locked the door and dropped her clutch, thigh holster, and tiny Colt onto the end table. Flipping off the torturous heels, she trudged past the cozy seating area and kitchenette.

Fluffy white cotton pillowed her reverse-swan-dive onto the bed. A shower was in order. The absence of his sexy musk would make the night easier, but she wasn't ready to let go just yet. Feet dangling over the edge, she tossed an arm over her eyes, and weathered the discord between her body and mind.

A *tap* sounded at the window.

On any other night, Harper would have lurched for her gun. Tonight, only one person was crazy enough to risk life and limb on her rusty fire escape. The only question was why?

She eased her arm from her face, and her head toward the window. Declan's frame clogged her twinkling city view. He'd removed his tie and coat. Sinewy forearms shown tan beneath rolled cuffs. In two fingers, he held a six-pack mix of Birra Moretti and Asahi Kuronama. Instead of a smile or smolder, his handsome face was set in neutral.

Her heart skittered. So she flung herself off the bed and stalked to the window. The rickety thing opened smoothly on an easy pull, because she was the only one crazy enough to dangle her feet through the railing and watch the city each night before bed.

Harper braced her hand on the frame, barring his entrance. "I'm not worth wining and dining or beering and fucking. As you can see." She flipped a hand toward the coffee table that doubled as a dining table. "There's no big payout."

When they hit the ledge, the beer bottles clinked together. Declan's hands wrapped her waist, and he plucked her off her feet.

She clutched his biceps for balance, then ducked as he hoisted her through the window.

"Payouts come in many forms, Harper." His hard chest pinned her to the brick. One hand skated to her ass for support while the other heated a path to her neck. Her legs dangled in thin air. "From what I've seen, this is my most justifiable risk-reward to date."

The words rumbled beneath his stout muscles, vibrating against her breast. A hint of champagne wafted off his breath as his lips drew near.

"How about you?"

Her conscience screamed, "No!" But her nipples beaded, and her clit pulsed against the tip of his erection. Harper bit her lips to keep from screaming, "Yes!" Her hands fisted in the starch of his shirt, and her body strained in defiance of her control.

"Why me?" Harper's head shook. "No, I know why. You're just trying to screw my case."

"You don't have a case. No one does. What I do is legend and morally reprehensible, but not illegal in most states or provinces." The middle of his brow pinched, and his tone dropped. "I'm trying to screw you, not your case."

He pressed her so hard with his body it forced the air from her lungs. "Yes," she whispered with the last of her breath.

His hands seized the split of her dress and yanked. The delicate material *shrieked*. Sultry night air blew across her bare cheeks. He levered back, but his expression elicited a gasp. Animalistic lust tensed his features. With practiced hands he hiked her onto his hips and guided her legs around his torso.

Harper moaned at the shock of full contact with his rigid girth.

"Kiss me, Harper. Show me you want this as much as I do. I'm desperate for you."

The silk of his hair tickled her fingers as she wound them full. She leaned to his mouth, inch by excruciating inch, knowing as soon as she made contact, there would be no turning back. He held himself taut, breathing as deeply as she. Their lips touched, mouths open in anticipation. Harper dragged her hands to his face, hiding the sweetness of their kiss from the world, and maybe herself.

Magnus's arms coiled around her back, holding her as firmly as the wall had. His hands splayed hot on her shoulders. She nestled her mouth, moving it this way and that, against his, relishing the feel. Firm and supple at the same time. Tender and harsh. Her tongue slipped inside, tasting.

One hand abandoned her while the other coasted to her bottom. She heard the swoosh of leather, the rasp of a zipper. A foil wrapper came next. Yet, his gaze remained absorbed on her. He sat on the narrow ledge, supporting them with his powerful legs. Without a word, he dragged her panties to the side, and positioned the thick head of his cock at the cleft of her slick channel.

When he eased her deliberately onto his shaft, Harper broke the kiss. She moaned as he filled her to the boundary of pleasure and pain.

His hands left her bottom and dove into her hair, framing her face. He nibbled her lower lip and breathed her deep. "God, Harper, touch me."

The pleading in his voice had her holding his face tighter and pulling him closer, though there was no part of her not touching him. Their mouths mated until her lips stung, and her body craved everything he had to offer. Slowly she leaned back, holding his gaze as her hands dropped to his buttons. Each loosened fastener revealed more slabs of muscle under snug skin that she explored with her fingers.

She tugged the shirt off his shoulders and clamped onto the bulging cords. One steady rock of her hips built onto another. Magnus held her face close, stripping her bare with his gaze—to her very soul—while she loved him with her body. There were no tricks of a seasoned pro seducing a woman. She'd seen them, knew he had them. But on the balcony in sight of a tiny chunk of Manhattan, only the two of them existed.

Harper arched. The position rubbed her breasts and clit against his hard body. Orgasm shook her from the inside out. She came with short pants and quiet mews. When the climax rose too high, her lids clamped shut and her body bowed.

Magnus attacked her neck with fierce kisses and scrapes of his teeth. He squeezed the globes of her ass in his hands, guiding her up and down his engorged penis. On the fourth stroke, his nails skewered her skin.

Harper's gaze found his as he pulsed his release deep

inside. His jaw strained and every muscle in his body coiled, but he didn't look away. Those vibrant blue eyes bore into her dark ones, just as they had in the bathroom.

He snugged a hand over hers, atop his strumming heart, and filled his lungs. Neither of them moved or said a word. Only held the moment as furiously as they could. When their breaths evened, he leaned forward and nibbled her collarbone while he shredded the rest of the most expensive garment she owned.

A giggle slipped from her lips as he tossed the spent material though the window. The laughter died the moment he lifted her heavy breasts to his mouth, basting each in eager praise.

His agile fingers dipped lower, slipping and swirling around her sensitive folds. "Kiss me and come for me, but don't let me go."

Hips rolling, she rode his still-rigid girth and trained hand. He stoked her little nub in the pinch of his thumb and forefinger. His other hand toyed with her distended nipple, while his lips roamed her chest.

A heat wave more fearsome than any a city-dweller had ever seen engulfed her. Flames danced behind her lids. Harper held tight to the dangerous spark, hugging him with every bit of strength her shaky body possessed. The strong, predatory swindler buried his face in her tresses, clasping her just as intensely.

Magnus blinked in the morning sun and wondered

how he'd slept through the city racket with the window open. When he stretched into the hot body next to him, he remembered in a wicked flash. Harper's long, onyx hair fanned over the pillow, nestling her angular and breathtaking features. Gone was the heavy make-up. He relished her fresh-faced serenity. Her tongue was sharp but honest. Endearing.

He knew familial love, but the love for a woman had been about as real as the Cubs winning the World Series in the next century. He didn't know if things would work between him and Harper past breakfast. But he knew even the potential of time with her, of affection, and something more was worth a try.

Rolling close, he draped one arm over her torso and snuck another under the pillow to tangle in her hands.

Her lashes fluttered open. The brackets of her thin lips etched in a smile that punched him in the gut. If he'd thought making love with her was something, waking with her was just as sweet.

"At the gallery," she whispered. "You didn't let her touch you."

"None have, except you. And you did it before your fingers grazed my skin."

The unmistakable *click-click* of hand-cuffs scratched his brain a moment before the chill of metal cinched around his pillow-covered wrist. Magnus tamped the spike of adrenaline at the thought of being caged. If Harper held the key, he might well enjoy the punishment. That was a big if. Would she relinquish him to the handful of people champing for his sun-dried pelt?

"So you're planning on keeping me?" Magnus smiled to camouflage his real concern. He wasn't a bad man. He wasn't a good one either. There were plenty of counts that would keep him behind bars long enough that he'd lose Harper. And her honor would let them. Hell, her morals might demand it. Damn ironic that the trait he most liked about her—besides her sweet ass and disarming smile—would be the one that sealed his fate.

"Oh, yes." Her brows waggled. The rounds of her cheeks and arching mouth knocked him back onto the pillow. A wrinkle worked its way between her brows. "I just can't decide for what: business or pleasure."

"Why not both?" he offered the Hail-Mary-long-shot of his lifetime, and that was saying something.

Her mouth opened, and then closed. She bore into his gaze with her own, searching for what, he didn't know, but hoped his walls dropped enough that she caught a glimpse of it. "I'm listening," she whispered.

Magnus cradled her cheek in his hand, beyond thankful to whatever god listened to his plea and determined to become a man worthy of the beauty in his embrace.

"Check out my story, Detective Lang. Whatever grievous charges stick, force me to work off my sentence here, with you."

Those dark eyes shifted back and forth. Weighing her career and morals against her lust and—just maybe—a piece of her heart. A breath whooshed past him laden with mint and a hint of sex.

"I don't know."

Magnus's lungs stung.

Pink lips formed a pout and Harper shrugged. "I do like the way you look in handcuffs."

His heart started beating again, and he pulled her mouth to his. More than willing for his advance, she rushed him. The tips of her fingers splayed across his cheeks and roamed his neck. A giggle spilled out onto his tongue and seeped into his soul. Hell, he'd try any look for her. Cuffs. Suits. Jeans. Even prison stripes. But he wouldn't let her know it. Not yet.

Opals

Axa Lee

WHEN HE THOUGHT of her, he tasted opals. One opal. The raw, uncut stone he'd stolen, carried in his mouth as he shimmied down the drainpipe and sprinted across the acres of dew-soaked lawns of the manse, to pay her blood price. But that had been a long time ago, when they were not who they were now. He thought of her often, climbed so high in the City Above. But from where he sat, even on a throne, such a height meant only a farther distance to fall.

The dark-haired girl in his bed, the one with the Goth eyes, rose and stumbled to her clothes. All the grift-girls wanted a turn with the Grif himself.

"My liege," she slurred as she left.

He had impressions of dark pubic hair, slim, supple muscles, jutting pink bitable nipples, and a tight pussy. She'd stagger down the steep, half-rotted tavern stairs and rejoin the party below, of thieves and pickpockets, connivers, dodgers, and their ladies. She'd drink and fuck and shriek her laughter, strident and loud, his spunk and that of others running down her leg.

She didn't interest him.

He rose, crossing the moon-lit room to the chair where his coat lay. Without disturbing the fabric, more from habit of practice than from necessity, he pulled the letter out of a pocket, though he already knew what it said. *Come to me*, written in cipher—the same code they'd used as children—the handwriting elegantly soaring and diving along the single page. The princess's own letterhead with flowers pressed into the paper as a watermark to prove its authenticity.

Come to me, the note said, and nothing else. But it didn't need to; she'd said where she wanted him, given him all the clues he needed to get there. He just didn't know what those clues were yet.

He looked out the tavern window to the City Above. The moon hung high above the city, shining large and luminous, hanging precariously over the castle spires of the City Above, as though it might be unhinged and crash to earth.

Opals.

She sent these missives sometimes, on various mediums, all in cipher, all meant as cryptic challenges, daring him to steal something, always the same thing—her. She wanted to be taken, desired, stolen. And he obliged. After all, she was his oldest friend. As the king's property, death was the result for any man who'd touch her, if he dared.

And he would dare, very much; he would dare.

And that's when he saw it.

"Oh, you brilliant little bitch," he said.

★ ★ ★

THE PALACE GUARDS slumped at their posts, asleep to a man in the darkness. The watch fires blazed away, unmonitored. The western wall was the highest and darkest of the various points of entry into the castle. Exactly why he had chosen it—as it was not only generally regarded as impossible to climb, but, as a result, the least guarded. After all, who wasted manpower on an impossible wall?

The City Above sat on a plateau, with the backside of the palace wall rising straight up from the sheer sides of the rock. The princess's tower, the second tallest tower, lay just beyond, an impossible span between the top of the wall and the wall of the tower for anyone who wasn't the king of thieves. He let himself relax into the climb, his soft-soled shoes pliable from years of use, his fingers nimble, finding cracks in the rock that no average man could have found let alone grip. But grip he did, spidering up the wall with a thief's grace. Most thieves would have utilized the dark of the moon, but even she had seen the folly in this. Too much darkness might hide one from the guards, but it would also hide hand and footholds from a thief. No—a partial moon, a waning moon with its paler light, provided sufficient moonlight, making him less apt to misjudge and fall to his death, and taking advantage of the laxness of lazy guards, too resigned in their position to expect a thief daring enough to attempt the climb.

He liked being where he was least expected.

After more than a little effort, he reached the window he sought and hauled himself bodily into the princess's rooms.

She was waiting there, staring into the fireplace, her mouth forming a soft 'O' of surprise. Then she smiled.

That cocksure grin that went straight to his groin. The same way it had ever since he'd first seen her as a woman when they were kids and not just another one of his mates running barefoot from the guards through the streets of the City Below.

"You came," she said, then cocked her head to the side with a roguish smile. "I was beginning to think it was too much of a challenge."

He threw down his fingerless gloves on the table like a challenge, and began stripping himself from the layers of clothing, meant to fold over themselves easily, so as to match the surroundings in any situation, tossing them all aside without a glance. "Woman, I just climbed thousands of feet up an impossible rock face, past guards armed to the teeth and ready to shove a sword through my gullet. I scaled the castle walls and into the top of the tallest bloody tower in the City Above." He spread his arms wide. "A little appreciation?"

"Second highest," she corrected. "And honestly? I think kingship's made you a little soft."

"Soft?" He crossed the space between them in three quick strides, one hand seizing her around the waist, the other slipping down the neckline of her gown. Then he pinched the nipple he found there, making her gasp and press herself against him. He nuzzled the soft flesh at the side of her neck. "I'm not the one with expensive soaps and the best perfumes." He kissed her throat, and she shivered under his mouth.

"Your king is asleep?" he asked.

She exhaled a breathy moan but managed a nod. Her eyelids fluttered. Her cheeks turned a high pink, the color she turned when he roused her the most. Her hair brushed her neck in little ringlets it must have taken her maid hours to create. Her lips were quickly bitten to a rush of pink color, and he longed to feel those lips wrapped around his cock.

"And the princess is away," she said.

For it was not the princess, but the monarch's mistress he held in his arms.

He groaned again, his hands moving roughly to her ribcage to squeeze and haul her against him, biting her earlobe as he did so. As she began to gasp, he loosened his hold and pulled back. She was the same striking beauty she'd always been with the same mischievous gleam in her eye, the same mouth any man who saw her pictured bobbing on his cock.

Come quickly, the note said, written in the cipher they'd used as children, when they called themselves the king of thieves and the queen of whores, still ignorant of what their futures held.

He set her back a bit with a groan, guiding her by her upper arms. "I'll need your money, luv, and that necklace." He tweaked the shining bauble at her throat. "This is my work on a night such as this."

She made to jerk away from him. His grip tightened. Her breathing quickened.

"You think me a common strup, content to service a man in a piss-stinking alley?"

"No, my lady," he said, dragging his lips along the column of her throat, making her shiver. "But at heart, I am a thief. Though not one who has ever left a woman unsatisfied once she's given up her blunt."

And with that he swept her from her feet and tumbled her onto the bed. She let out a girlish shriek entirely unbecoming a king's mistress, but one that completely suited the girl he remembered, the tangle-haired street urchin who swam in the city harbor, dodged the city guard, raced through the streets barefoot, and sunbathed on rooftops. Then came a low-throated, sultry chuckle that left nothing of the girl and spoke of everything she had learned since.

Lying back, propped up on her elbows, she gazed up at him, eyes hooded, mouth smiling, looking happier than he'd ever seen her. He took his time, kissing his way up her long bare legs, making her shiver as his mouth approached her wet, swollen cunt at a glacial pace.

She sighed as he approached her inner thighs, shivering with expectation. She grabbed his hair, attempting to draw him into her more quickly.

Instead he bypassed her sweet spot and moved to look eye-to-eye. He stroked back her hair, searching in her face for... what? What did he expect to find there? What he did find was a soft green-eyed gaze looking back, all playfulness gone, leaving only a genuine tenderness.

"I missed you," she whispered.

He tried to convince himself he imagined the tenderness as she sat up, tracing her tongue around his ear, before biting lightly on the lobe to draw him down. She took his face between her hands, drawing him farther down to be lost amidst a voluminous gown and sumptuous bedclothes, as though drowning in cotton and silk, that sultry chuckle all around him.

And that easily the tone of their lovemaking changed from violent, almost desperate, to something slower, sultrier, almost tender.

Their lovemaking often started out so—brutal, aggressive, not violent but certainly assertive. Sometimes, it was she, there and ready with a blindfold and stack of chains. Other times, he was the one to bind her. But lately the tenor had changed, often beginning with posturing and domination, but culminating with an almost-gentle quality that left them both shaken and quiet. Gradually, no more toys, no more props appeared between them, only his body and hers, and the quiet gasps and sighs, the nail marks running down his back, the slightly reddened ass cheeks of her, to show for their efforts.

This time was no different, the initially aggressive actions slowing, softening, into something far less showy and possessing far more depth.

He stroked a hand up her smooth thigh, coming to rest on the rounded swell of her ass. He dug in his fingers, making her arch and moan against him. She had always liked a firm hold on her ass, and by her reaction, practiced or not, it'd been a long time since a man had grabbed her the way she liked. He licked and stroked and made her come in a dozen small ways until he felt her growing more restless, eager for more than just his fingers and tongue.

He rolled onto his back, drawing her over him, his cock resting at the juncture of her thighs.

"Don't tease me," she gasped, her slickness writhing on his hard length, her face flush and pink.

He eased into her, slowly, holding her hips to prevent her moving too quickly.

"Wait," he soothed. "Go slow."

"I can't... I..." She was already rocking, shaking, fairly vibrating with her need for his touch.

He groaned and gave in, plunging into her fully, rocking their pelvises together, his mouth trembling with effort. And then she was coming, so hard and so fast it was all he could do to keep up with her, thrusting into her, urging her on, until her own pleasure broke, her pussy clenching his cock with an almost painful fervor...until the spasms passed. He drew her down onto his chest, holding her tightly to him as her heart hammered inside of her chest.

He kissed her ear, her cheek, rubbed her back, reminding her to slow her breathing. And gradually she came back to herself, coherent but spent, not even protesting when he allowed her to slide off his still partially erect cock, her body slack from orgasm, while his had yet to spurt its final pleasure. But he found he had no need. He enjoyed her enough as it was; he had no need to come every time.

She rested on her side in the circle of his arm, her hand resting on the center of his chest.

It was then he noticed it. He examined the ring on her finger.

"He wants to marry me off," she said. "Respectability and all that."

"And?" he said. "Isn't that what you wanted?" By the intense look on her face, he knew it wasn't.

"I wanted money, that look on a man's face when you know you've got him. And I have those things. It all just got so…"

"Easy?"

She looked up at him. "Yes."

She'd finally put word to the very thing that had been bothering him as well. He'd clawed and climbed and killed his way to become the highest among the city's lowest, a king among thieves, the Grif himself. But as the baubles and coin and swag came his way, he found life easier and the booty less satisfying. He'd feared even putting a name to this discontent he'd felt building over the past months, but lying there, with her, he found he knew exactly what she meant. Life at the top had gotten too easy, it seemed, for both of them.

She sat up. "It just seems so…boring."

"I'd hardly call a climb up an unclimbable wall boring, darlin'," he said. But deep down he knew what she meant.

"I can have anything, have any man I want," she was saying. "And I stand there at these grand parties, surrounded by dukes and earls and their luscious, well-preserved wives and...I don't want any of them. I don't want any of it."

"We could add some flogging," the Grif suggested, but the Queen shrugged it off.

"I'm not talking about a little slap and tickle," she said. "I'm talking about honest to gods boredom. I mean, I walk into one of these parties, and I know I could have any man I wanted, and half the women. It's...frightfully dull. I want..." She laughed. "I want hot haddock, fried fresh with salt just off Market Street, and sold so piping hot the salt burns into your fingers when the old woman tosses it to you."

"The old woman died," he said. "Her daughter runs it now."

"See, that's what I mean!" She sat up, facing him. "I'm locked up here, and I'm missing everything. And then he'll marry me off, and I'll miss even more. I want to see mountains again and feel the sun on my face lying on rooftops above the bazaar. I want to go down to the public baths and not have to take fifteen serving women along to wipe my ass."

He laughed.

She threw a pillow his way, but she was laughing as well. "I'm serious! I want to stand at the prow of a ship and feel the sea spray on my face. I want to let the rain and wine run down my face, to press grapes with my feet. I want to climb to the top of a watchtower and gaze out across the sea. I want to ride with a caravan where there's nothing for miles and miles but sweet grass and the farts of mules."

"To freeze in winter, and starve in summer."

"To riffle the stores of the greatest sultan…"

"To dodge the soldiers…"

"To see great paintings…"

"To stand with our hands on the block for stealing them…"

"To fuck wherever we please."

He pulled her down to him, biting her lip, hands tight on her upper arms, her laughter against his mouth. And for a moment he wanted her, he wanted it, so badly that it made an ache inside of him.

And then he came back to himself. "We've worked hard for what we have, love," he said, setting her away again. "To get where we are. Is that not enough? You'd give all that up?" He smiled, but he couldn't make the expression reach his eyes.

Her clear green gaze met his. "Wouldn't you?"

Even now, after all the time apart, she still picked him apart and left his game shattered on the floor. She could name his deepest desires and greatest fears and strip them bare.

He drew her down to his chest, her fingers spread against the stiff black hairs there, lips inches from his own. He nuzzled her neck. "I will be needing that necklace, sweet," he said, his fingers snaking toward the clasp.

She slapped away his hand. "Like hell."

There was the street-savvy girl he remembered. Easy life had softened her, but not worn her away completely. "All your money and the necklace. That is my work on a night such as this."

Lightning danced in the sky behind him as he spoke. A storm was coming. And he wanted to be away before it broke over the cities.

She toyed with the pendant, thoughtfully rolling it between her fingers in a gesture that seemed as though she must do it often. "I go where it goes."

"Are you asking me to take you away from here?"

She grinned. "I'm asking you to let me use your rope."

And she rolled off, bouncing as her feet hit the stone floor. She fetched a bag from the corner, tugging it open to pull out dark clothes of various colors—thieves' clothes—and began to pull them on.

"You're not coming with me." He rose from the bed as well, tying his breeches back on and fetching his shoes.

"The hell I'm not," she replied, tying back her hair as she headed for the balcony. She was reaching for his rope, throwing her leg over the lip of the rail, looking out at the storm gathering along the far horizon.

"The hell you are. Get off that rope. Don't you dare climb down the side of that... no, hey! I'm talking here!"

She looked up at him. "A beautiful, sexually talented woman wants to run away with you in the middle of the night, and you're saying no?"

"Woman, I'm the king of thieves; I can make away with any woman I want."

She shrugged. "Go ahead then. But be sure to bring her home when you return. For future reference, I'm partial to blondes." She winked and vanished over the edge of the balcony.

He stood there a moment, taking it all in. The King of Thieves, the Grif himself, tamed by a saucy, red-haired wench? Well, not just any wench, the Queen of Whores herself. And over the years, hadn't they made quite a team? He smiled to himself, thinking of the jobs they'd pulled, before either of them was remotely underworld royalty. If he was honest with himself, he missed those days—the scurrying through streets and up the sides of buildings, the scams and grifts and heists. He'd missed her smile and spunky wit. And now, here she was, giving him a chance at that life again. Could he really pass that up out of pride?

"Are you coming?"

He smiled and reached for the rope, expertly swinging himself over the side and slithering down.

He'd heard Morocco was nice. Maybe he'd take her to Morocco. A Sultan lived in Morocco as well, fabled to be very rich indeed...

Her Heart's Tomb

Jennifer Kacey

THE GROUND RUMBLED beneath Sonya's feet, and she held her breath. Nearly half a mile inside the burial chamber with her arm poised in the air and her finger on the trigger of an aerosol can, what she needed least was a freaking earthquake to put a quick end to this expedition.

Several seconds later, the warm tomb quieted, and all she could hear was the *thump-thump* of her heartbeat. Losing her focus in front of an empty room shouldn't have kicked her heart into overdrive, but she'd bet her bounty the room wasn't empty at all.

Depressing the knob on the can of her least favorite body spray, she smiled.

The three-foot expanse in front of her lit up with a complex grid of nearly invisible threads, each now revealed by the aerosolized liquid clinging to the fibers. Empty room, her ass. But when she drew in a satisfied breath, the scent of the Axe spray hit her—his scent—nearly taking her to her knees.

Jack.

"Fuck," she whispered to her broken heart. "He's not coming. He doesn't give a shit. This is my tomb. Mine."

Shrugging off her pack along with the nostalgia, she set the can on the ground at her feet. She slipped as many of her things as she might need into the pockets of her cargo pants and again faced the room.

Thankfully, open spaces at the top of the rock cavern allowed enough light in to illuminate the area she needed to work. Infiltrate? Break into? Whatever. Some people worked in an office space or a clothing store. She wasn't most people.

Tucking her long dark braid into the back of her tank top, she readjusted her firearm holster and palmed the butt of her custom-made handgun. The one Jack made.

Equal parts lust and hurt filled her chest as she thought about receiving the gift.

She choked off the emotions and bent to snatch the deodorant spray off the rock floor. One of the only reminders of him she had. One of the two things he'd left in their apartment before he'd bugged out. The other thing he'd left? A note in his halting scrawl saying he had to leave. He loved her, needed her, but he couldn't stay and couldn't explain why.

Again spraying the area in front of her, she tried to forget him and moved with purpose. Not slow, not quick. She didn't dare rush as she weaved through the mesh of trip wires. Hurrying through a booby trap would turn her into another of the skeletons she'd seen crumpled along the way. Lesser men had fallen before her.

Good riddance.

A woman was smaller, lither, and could get in and out of tighter spaces and circumstances than a man ever could. Jack had commented on it several times. His praise? She hated to admit it, but she trusted his words.

Trusting wasn't something she did easily. But she'd trusted Jack. Trusted him enough, loved him enough, to teach him what she knew. Stealing for the highest bidder wasn't a particularly noble profession, but thieving was what she knew. Her parents were the notorious international jewel thieves of Taipei. At last count, they were wanted on four continents.

Spraying upward again, she maneuvered through the last section of filaments, and then pocketed the can of spray.

Jewels.

So limiting.

As she was on her own, she'd branched out. Art work, statues, vehicles, artifacts. One-of-a-kind treasures—like the item she was hunting now—were her favorite. She'd steal anything except for three things: drugs, arms, or people. She wouldn't touch those jobs.

Around a corner, she wiped her brow, thankful for the lack of a draft, or Jack's spray wouldn't have done her any good before. Any wind movement through the tunnels would have dispersed the spray too quickly, and the liquid couldn't have collected on the threads. Maybe luck was on her side. Or fate was faking her out, getting ready to kick her ass again.

Checking her watch, she calculated how much longer she'd have daylight. Ninety minutes at most then she'd have to abort. Getting trapped in a tomb with no light and plummeting temperatures would seal the deal on a shitty month.

As she quietly moved along the corridor, Sonya let her mind wander back to the man who'd left her weeks ago. The day had started like many others. Early that morning, he'd woken her. Her favorite way. Rolling her onto her stomach and moving between her thighs. Fucking her slow, deep. Hard.

His deep voice in her ear, whispering for her to come for him. To come on his cock.

Across their moonlit loft back in the States stood a freestanding mirror, reflecting their love-making. Her much-darker skin tone—thanks to her Egyptian ancestry—beneath his much-lighter, European complexion. The visual they made together stole her breath.

For the first few strokes, she'd always wonder if she were dreaming. Because no man felt that good inside her, and not just her pussy. He was inside *her*, part of her, and they'd been together for almost a year.

In the dark was when he'd sneaked inside her heart. When all of her defenses were down, and he'd asked her about her dreams and wishes. Things she'd never shared with anyone.

The one and only man to whom she'd ever said the words, "I love you."

He'd said it back. And that was supposed to mean something, right?

But that was then, and this was now. Amazing how different life could be after finding her "Dear Sonya" letter almost a month ago.

Shaking her head, she focused on the next obstacle, happy to have her attention drawn to something that would kill her quickly. Rolling bars of spikes that spun over a pit filled with… Peering over the edge, she grabbed her penlight from a pocket and clicked it on.

Snakes. A pit filled with snakes. Thankfully, Sonya had no issues with the slithering reptiles. Well. As long as they weren't the two-legged variety.

After successfully crossing to the other side of the pit, Sonya pictured the treasure she sought. A small black stone the size of her palm. A stone supposedly stolen hundreds of years before from the very tomb of Qin Shi Huang, the first Chinese emperor. The Peruvian tomb she trekked through held its secret, but if Sonya had her way, it wouldn't much longer.

People seeking her services called her a tomb raider. Her business cards stated she was simply an *Artifact Recovery Specialist*. That she'd never failed a job made her card quite valuable. A card only passed in the most elite circles and only to people who could meet her asking price, which contained quite a few zeroes.

Money spoke many languages, and her current client was quite…fluent.

Why they wanted the black stone she wasn't certain, but her research had turned up the fact the stone wasn't common at all, but rather a rare black diamond worth enough to purchase a sizeable country.

Another open section of corridor loomed in front of her. Goose bumps rose on her skin. The quiet surrounding her wasn't serene. The eerie pause reminded her of the silences that fell over forests when danger closed in. Animals always knew when something horrible grew close.

The feeling of being watched crawled up her neck. A glance behind her revealed nothing. She should have had a partner along, watching her back. Hating to admit she missed Jack's presence didn't make her feel any better.

Her gaze went back to the flooring in front of her. A strange pattern carved into the stone caught her eye. Something she'd seen before. It was never good. Crouching low, she grabbed a handful of loose gravel and sand and tossed it at the ground in front of her. Spikes recessed in the wall shot across the space in front of her. Throwing more rocks proved there were more darts to be tripped—some high, some low. A few even shot out from the ceiling.

That was new.

She would have been impressed if it wasn't her hide on the line.

Several more handfuls of debris tossed before her produced nothing. Decisively, she moved across the floor, ready to jump out of the way at any time, but it seemed lady luck was still with her. Very unfulfilling company, in her opinion.

Around another curve, she stopped. A rock wall spanned the entire twenty-foot height of the tomb. A door in the middle was its only adornment.

Cautiously, she checked the edges, handle, and the floor in front of it.

Nothing.

Her neck tingled again. Not as if anyone could sneak up on her anyways. Jack had always told her she had eyes in the back of her head.

Invading thoughts, when she needed to stay hyper-aware of what she faced, pissed her off. Taking one deep breath after another, she cleared her mind to concentrate on what she hoped would be the final barrier between herself and her treasure. She'd been searching for months. Once she found it and delivered it safely to her buyer, she'd take the other half of her payout and decide whether or not she had the heart to stay in the game any longer. Always having to be on the move took more of a toll than she cared to admit.

Completing her examination of the door, she determined she needed to drill a hole in the wood to see what was on the other side. But she didn't have the right tools.

Fuck it. If something was set to detonate on opening, which was her guess, then she'd just have to improvise or kiss her ass goodbye. But then, going out in a fireball of glory had always sounded appealing. Fate had her number either way, and she had no other option.

She tried the handle, even knowing it would be locked. Then a thought struck her, and she smiled.

From beneath her tank top, she pulled a long chain and an ancient-looking key. She didn't even want to think about how much money it had cost to find this key. Nor how much trouble it had been to procure. And especially not the fact it was the last mission Jack and she had completed together.

Removing the key from around her neck, heart kicking against her ribs, she slid it into the lock and turned. The latching mechanism released with a tiny snick.

Moment of truth.

Sonya gripped the door handle, rotating it slowly, taking in each degree of movement for any indication something was rigged to blow. The tumbler snapped free of the frame, and she opened the door a tiny fraction of an inch.

A grenade from the last century was rigged to the door. A string tied to the ring of the detonation pin connected to something on the other side of the door she couldn't see. Keeping one hand on the handle, she fished out a pair of cutters. They were barely thin enough to fit through the narrow space, but they did the trick.

Pocketing the cutters, she pushed the door open farther, and thankfully glanced up at the last possible moment to see another trap rigged at the top of the doorframe. The back of her neck tingled once more, so she made the choice to leave the trap set in case someone tried to surprise her. Keeping the key, she left the door unlocked in case she needed to run for it. Fading light told her she needed to hurry.

A skeleton lay slumped on the floor to her left with tattered rags covering bone. Unfortunately, she'd never know his story since he was long since dead. But her curiosity was aroused. Every mystery deserved an investigation, but she had a job to complete.

Inside, treasure of various kinds littered the floor and walls. Every surface was covered with coins and jewels, but the black stone was nowhere.

"Sonya."

In the span of a heartbeat, she swiveled to face the door, her weapon aimed directly at the heart of the intruder. "Jack…"

As the door swung open, she homed in on her target and pulled the trigger.

Jack shouted, and Sonya closed her eyes, praying she'd made the right decision.

"You fucking shot at me."

His deep voice sent shivers down her spine, landing on her clit, which did a happy dance at his presence.

Didn't take her two extra seconds to get royally pissed off that any part of her was pleased about his presence. She thought about shooting him for real, but she shoved her handgun back into her holster and latched it into place before she could change her mind. "I never miss. If I'd wanted you dead, you'd be piled up with Casper over there." She jabbed a thumb in the dead guy's general direction and went back to searching for the diamond.

"If you weren't shooting at me, then what were you shooting at?"

His growled timbre thrilled part of her and made the rest want to weep at how much she'd missed it. "Trip line. Top of the door. Wired to a gas canister on the wall filled with who knows what toxic cocktail. You open the door anywhere past halfway, yank the cord, and we become history. Classic rookie mistake," she scoffed. "I'm pretty sure I taught you better than that."

Keeping her face free of emotion, not to mention the damn tears in check, wouldn't last long. Finding her treasure would save her in more ways than one. She moved cautiously, checking for more traps, but the room seemed free from any more death and destruction. And death from a broken heart was totally not a thing. At all. Ever.

"Why didn't you disable it when you came through?"

Genuine hurt bled across the room to her, and she gritted her teeth. She mostly shook it off. And knocked over a gold goblet sitting on a stone shelf. "I knew someone was following me. Could have been anyone. So I left it alone. I'd rather be dead than caught."

The sun was rapidly setting, and the last thing she wanted was to be trapped in the tomb overnight with the man who'd broken her heart.

"You can speak so flippantly of death?"

"Just another adventure," as her parents said years before they died on a hunt.

Glancing his way was a bad choice. Tall and broad-chested and wearing a middle-eastern headdress and cargo pants that matched hers, his lighter skin tone made him look like some European sheik. Without a shirt to cover his pecs. Nothing could keep her mind from thinking of the last time she'd seen it bare. Him inside her, protecting her, keeping her safe.

For what?

So he could disappear the next morning with no explanation?

Fuck. That.

Mindless conversation of how he wrecked her by leaving? Sounded fun. She could do that. Totally. If her hands would stop shaking, and she could quit knocking shit over, her mask of indifference might be believable.

Looking again, he'd moved closer, but thankfully wasn't staring at her anymore. He glanced at his watch, then huffed out a frustrated breath as he stared upward at the waning light. Then he took up her mantle, searching through piles to find what they'd come for.

Ugh.

She'd come for the diamond. Not him. Not anymore. Partners didn't abandon each other.

"I didn't abandon you."

Jesus, Mary, and oh hell to the no. Talking out loud when she didn't mean to. Great.

"Will you at least let me explain before you write me off for good?" He'd moved closer, and now his baby blues were trained right on her.

Walking away, she wasn't exactly retreating. She just wanted to look for the diamond in another section of the cavern. She stopped mid-step and he almost slammed into her back. "Casper," she whispered.

"Soooo, is that a yes or no on me explaining?" His voice faded as she ran across the stone floor and hit the floor on her knees in front of the skeleton lying on his side beside the door.

Carefully, she adjusted the bones, wondering if another trap was set. The remains of the person before her fell apart, and she sifted through them until she found a perfect fist, clutching—a black stone. "The Devil's Heart," she whispered.

"How'd you know he had it?" Jack was right behind her as she unlocked the dead man's hand from around the diamond and stood.

"Casper could be a woman." Being in a man's typical line of work, she couldn't help but point that out as she held the jewel up to one of the last shafts of sunlight streaming in the cave. A spectacular prism of color appeared on the far wall. No matter the circumstances, she couldn't help but stop for a moment of pure awe at its beauty.

"Touché."

Slipping the treasure in her pocket, she zipped it up and headed out the open door. Sweat ran between her breasts, and she was more than certain it had nothing to do with temperature. "Any treasure hunter would want to die with this treasure in his hands. If he got this far, he was a damn fine raider. And I heard two keys to the room existed. Guess I know where the second ended up."

At the wall of darts, she threw gravel and tripped another round of poisoned barbs.

"Why didn't he get out? Why stay?"

She picked up one of the tiny sticks of death as they moved toward the next obstacle. "Poisoned is my guess." Holding it up for Jack to see, she waited a second then tossed it back down.

He whistled. "You were born to be a raider. In the blood."

"In the blood," she said with him at the same time. It was a phrase her parents had taught her. One that she'd passed along to him. It reminded her of how close they'd become and how much she'd shared with him. How much she'd been looking forward to a life together. She'd even thought about retiring, maybe starting a family.

Rolling her eyes, she felt every bit as lame as she had when she'd realized he'd left. Never again would she let a man wield that kind of power over her.

Silence expanded between them as they made their way back across the spiked logs. The hissing snakes beneath their feet fit her mood perfectly.

"Aren't you going to talk to me at all?"

"No."

"You're not curious? I have a lot that I need to tell you." He understood her well enough to know he was asking a rhetorical question. "Come on, Sonya. We need to talk. Now. Cut me some slack."

Right before the web of trip wires, she wheeled on him, jabbing him in the chest he was so close. "I don't have to cut you anything. You bailed. With no explanation. I owe you noth—"

His lips found hers, and his hands dug into her hair, holding her to his body as he plundered her mouth.

The flavor of him. It intoxicated each of her senses, drowning her in pure sensation in less than the lifespan of a lit det cord. He wiped her mind blank, replacing the feeling of abandonment with longing and need.

His kiss engulfed her as his tongue slid into her mouth, taking what he wanted and giving in return. Love. He tasted like love and passion as he hauled her even closer.

His heat sent ripples of desire to her core, and moisture slid along the lips of her pussy. His hand on her breast, pinching her nipple, made her cry out. Her moan echoed off the walls of the passageway, jarring her out of her lust.

She shoved him away, nearly falling on her ass as she tried to find her footing. He placed a hand on her shoulder to steady her, but she threw it off. "Don't touch me."

She meant for it to sound harsh, abrasive. Instead, her words sounded downright sorrowful.

His eyes softened as he gazed at her. "I'm sorry. Shouldn't have done that. But I missed you." He held up his hands. "I won't touch you again, but we need to talk. I have something you have to hear."

Straightening her shoulders, she moved along the hall, fumbling in her pocket for her—his—*whatever*—spray. The filaments were invisible again, so she repeated the spray-shuffle-crawl procedure.

Luckily, the progress was slow, and they both had to concentrate to keep from being caught on anything. Even better, she moved quicker and was out the other side before he was halfway through. Grabbing her pack, she fled.

"Wait, Sonya. Wait!!"

Fat chance of that. She had nothing to say to him as she ran down the hall.

Running from him? Probably.

She'd beat herself up about it later. Right then, all she wanted was to get away from him *and* her need to go back and hear what he had to say. Because she couldn't let whatever excuse he had bend her will.

With the last of the light, she turned the final corner into what she knew was her salvation. The exit was right—

She screeched to a halt, nearly falling in her attempt to stay upright.

Huffing breaths wheezed out as she stared at the entrance. What was once the opening was now blocked with rock. Which made this space her burial tomb.

"Sonya!" Jack jogged up behind her. "I can explain."

"The rumble. When I was inside about to go through the trip wires, I felt a rumble. I thought it was an earthquake. But it wasn't, was it? This is what I felt. You triggered the door to blow when you came through. You missed the first trap."

"I was trying to tell you, but you wouldn't listen."

To add insult to injury, the last of the light faded quickly from the slots carved in the rock walls too high for them to reach or escape through. Darkness would move in quickly, and they'd have no choice but to spend the night trapped in the tomb, before they could attempt to free themselves at the first light of dawn.

"Let me explain."

His hand on her shoulder didn't last long as she

pivoted and punched him once straight across the jaw.

Groaning, he took a step back and rubbed his jaw.

The need to hit him again raced down her arm, but she shook out her fist as it started to throb. "Told you I never miss."

★ ★ ★

Hours later, the sound of her teeth chattering together bounced off the walls of the cavern where they decided to bunk down for the night. She'd already accused him of intentionally setting off the trap just to keep her in the tomb. He'd denied it. She didn't believe him.

"You're being stubborn, Sonya. Dying to teach me a lesson isn't the way to go about getting back at me."

She was so cold ice water sounded warm as she huddled in her too-thin sleeping bag. She was thankful for any protection against the rocks beneath her. Croaking before she conceded to sharing body heat with the man on the other side of the hall appealed as well. "I'm n-n-not trying to g-g-get back at y-you." Mostly.

She was hurt. The emotion was different. And stranded, so she couldn't run. Neither feeling really did it for her as she tried in vain to warm her hands again.

Unable to build a fire, to avoid revealing their position, they were limited to their sleeping bags, clothes, and the memory of being warm since Sonya was unwilling to bed down with her former lover.

"Fuck it." With jerky movements, Jack unzipped his sleeping bag and got to his feet. His shadow danced across the tomb walls from the battery-operated lamp positioned between them.

"D-don't come over h-h-h-here."

"The choice isn't up to you anymore, sweetheart."

Sweetheart. His pet name for her. Something she'd ached to hear again in his absence. Now it did nothing but rankle her already frayed nerves. Warmth spread through her middle, and she cursed beneath her breath as he moved his belongings to her side of the passageway. "It sure as s-s-shit is."

"Hush. I love you. I'm not letting you freeze to death." He covered her with his sleeping bag and unzipped hers.

Completely and utterly frozen, she was unable to move even a finger as he slipped inside her sleeping bag.

Not from the cold, though.

From his words. Three of them to be exact.

He zipped himself in, pulling his bag over their heads. Then he gathered her close, pillowing an arm beneath her head.

Shaking, he held her quaking body and kissed her hair. His warmth seeped inside her, wrapping her in a safe cocoon.

Until that moment, she hadn't realized how lost she'd been without him. His closeness thawed more than her body, and her emotions over spilled as he held her. Tears tightened her throat, and she had to swallow twice before speaking. "How c-can you say that to m-m-me?" Knowing she'd hate herself when the sun rose wouldn't stop the words from tumbling out. "Love? You speak of l-l-love, yet you have no idea what the word means."

"It means everything and nothing."

"You're making no s-sense. Maybe you're the one who needed to get warm." She snuggled closer, finally remembering what it was like to be able to feel her limbs.

His palm cupped her cheek, guiding her face upward so he could kiss her forehead, the tip of her nose, her mouth. Moving her lips apart, he took command of the kiss, stroking his tongue against hers until her entire body jerked beside him. The only time that happened was when she was on the verge of coming for him.

He'd barely touched her, certainly nothing below the waist, and yet, she couldn't deny how he called to her body. It was as much a traitor as her heart—already willing to forgive him if it meant he'd touch her and kiss her until the ache stopped hurting.

"It's everything because you filled each moment I was gone." His fingers tore at her tank to pull it over her head, and then attacked the button and zipper on her pants before shoving them off along with her panties.

On the verge of objecting, she realized she already had the shirt he'd donned shoved up to his armpits and the fly of his pants open, and she was stroking the thick shaft of his cock. "And nothing? Why was it nothing?" She gave up fighting her need for him and immersed herself in his scent, his touch, his—love. Licking his chest, she raised her top leg, throwing it over his thigh as he urged her legs apart.

"Fuck, I can smell how wet you are for me." His fingers dipped between her thighs, sliding in the wetness only he could elicit. One finger and then another filled her channel as his thumb slid across her pulsing clit. "And nothing, because that is what I am without you."

"But you left with no explanation." She stroked him in time as he filled her and panted against his mouth.

He pulled his fingers free just long enough to rid himself of his pants, and then he rolled her onto her back. Moving between her legs, he pushed her thighs wide and shoved in deep. Not in one painful thrust, but a handful of powerful drives to stretch her sex to accommodate him. "To protect you. I got word the buyer for the Devil's Heart was going to double-cross you. In case I was wrong and I was killed, I didn't want you to know anything about it. Plausible deniability, if you were questioned."

"I don't need protecting," she panted as she clawed at his back, arching to get closer. The tips of her nipples brushed his chest, and she moaned. Strings of pleasure connected her nipples to her clit, and she licked his chest, scraping her teeth along his flesh. She wanted her mark on him, just as surely as her back and ass would wear the marks of his passion from the rocks beneath her. He drove into her, faster and harder. His fist in her hair held her in place, and her pussy fluttered around him.

He shoved his free hand beneath them; she thought he meant to cushion her from the rocks. She opened her mouth to tell him he needn't worry, but a groan of pure delight came out instead. One of his fingers gathered her wetness then circled the pucker of her ass. He worked it inside, stretching her. A bite of pain. A bite of pleasure.

"You're mine to protect. It's the deluxe package you signed up for when you told me you loved me."

Hearing the honesty in his voice ripped away the last layer that separated them. His erection dragged across the swollen nub of her clit, and her pussy and ass clamped down on him as she came.

Her moan rebounded off the chamber walls as he filled her core. His cock jerked inside her as he sealed his lips over hers. Time stopped as she gave herself over to him again. Pleasure passed between them, magnified by their love, by her forgiveness.

Every ounce of her sucked at him greedily, wanting every drop of his seed because it was hers. Jolting, her spine shuddered as he pulled free. First from her ass then her pussy. Gathering her close, he rolled over until she lay on top of him.

He took her weight and held her tightly as their bodies finally relaxed.

She knew sleep was moments from claiming her, but she had something to say. "Don't think I've totally forgiven you for AWOLing on me. No matter how noble the reasoning."

"I wouldn't dream of assuming I'm off your shit list, my tomb raider."

His satisfaction danced all around her. The sun would warm them as a new day dawned. And with the Devil's Heart in her bag, they'd dig their way out and find their future. A new beginning with the man she loved by her side for the next adventure…

The Highwayman's Treasure

Emma Jay

JULIA VERITY DRIFTED around the table piled with cakes, wafers, and grapes, tugging at the neckline of her borrowed gown. If she were a better seamstress, she could have taken in the garment at the bust, though it would still sag at the waist. Of course, the garment was a horrid shade of lavender, not the least bit flattering to her red hair and freckles, so altering it might convey the idea that it belonged to her, when it was simply borrowed from her sister-in-law. Since Julia was now out of mourning, she had nothing appropriate for a ball. After Neville's death, she depended on the generosity of his sister. And avoided the leers of her brother-in-law, Joseph.

Naturally, that generosity had a price, and this week, the price was to escort her niece to the ball.

She wasn't chaperoning so well. She'd escaped the ballroom through the French doors and lingered near the food, even though she wasn't hungry. She was, however, quite weary of the pitying looks sent her by the members of the *ton* who had known and loved her husband. The comments were even worse—how much they missed him, what a good man he was. All true, except that he'd died young and left her penniless, childless, and at the mercy of his family.

Briefly, she wondered whether her sister-in-law had sent her to the ball so she might meet someone, but no, not in this dress. It would be in her sister-in-law's interest, getting her married and out of the house, wouldn't it? Maybe after she was finished playing governess for their three daughters.

Only the first was out in society, so that task would last a while.

She felt like she was being watched, and then looked up to meet an amused blue gaze over the plate of tea cakes. A jolt went through her. She hadn't seen Lucian, Neville's best friend, since the funeral mass. Before Neville died, Lucian had been a fixture in their home, and she'd felt his loss almost as keenly as Neville's. The first remark to her lips was to accuse him, to ask why he'd stayed away, but no. This was neither the time nor place.

"I see Angelica is treating you especially well," he said without preamble, his gaze sliding down her ill-fitting gown.

The glance reminded her their relationship had been too informal when Neville had been alive, and she had to remind herself they no longer had that relationship. She had to maintain her reputation or risk losing her place in Angelica's home. "Mr. Villaret," she said simply.

His eyebrow winged upward, and his lips twitched.

So handsome. He and Neville had been a striking pair, drawing the gazes of men and women alike anywhere they went: Neville, tall and blond; Lucian, dark-haired and broad-shouldered.

"So formal, Julia. Are you upset with me?"

"Why ever would I be?" Only that he'd disappeared from her life almost as completely as Neville. Not once had he called to see how she fared. Or to mourn Neville's loss with her.

He angled his head, his eyes losing that twinkle. "I'm sorry. Angelica is not a particular fan. She blames me for Neville getting into trouble."

Julia knew both men played an equal part, but that knowledge didn't help her forgive his abandonment. Still, she couldn't hide her curiosity. "I'm surprised to see you here. You ordinarily avoid balls this late in the season."

Grasping mamas looking for a match for their debutantes, he'd said. He wasn't a great catch as the younger son of a baron, but he was strikingly handsome, especially tonight in the crisp white shirt and dark coat, the snug-fitting breeches beneath. A stir of something she hadn't felt in over a year, had never expected to feel again, rose, and she looked past him, seeking an escape.

The twinkle returned, and he leaned closer. "I'm on the prowl."

She drew back, surprised at his vulgarity. "Lucian."

"Will you save me a dance?"

She hadn't danced since Neville died, and though she was out of mourning, she couldn't imagine doing so now. "I'm chaperoning my niece. Dancing wouldn't be appropriate."

He leveled his gaze at her. "Would it not?"

He saw too much. "I should get back. I'm not being a very effective chaperone."

"I'll escort you." He lifted his arm in invitation. "And perhaps you can introduce me to your niece."

He parted from her soon after, and she caught sight of him, dancing with several debutantes, one after another. She hated how she followed his actions on the dance floor, that she was fascinated by the interactions he had with these women—most of them no more than children, when he was a man of the world. She had been fortunate to wed a man close to her own age, and they had grown up together. That was another of the reasons she missed Neville so deeply.

She turned her attention from Lucian and watched her niece, Constance, who had less success finding partners. Julia would have felt sorry for the girl, but her niece took after her mother in temperament, which made sympathizing difficult.

★ ★ ★

"STAND AND DELIVER!"

The words, accompanied by the wobble of the carriage as the horses staggered to a stop, tumbled Julia from her seat and jolted her from the dread of returning to Angelica's house and Joseph's advances. She gripped the window and looked out into the night to see a masked man on a black horse in the middle of the road. His cape billowed behind him and his broad-brimmed hat shadowed his face, but the gun he waved was very visible.

She shrank back and put her arm around her niece, who stiffened at the contact.

"We have nothing, sir," the coachman said in a shaky voice.

"I know that not to be true. You have just come from a ball, have you not? The ladies within are bejeweled."

Constance made a high-pitched sound into Julia's neck.

Julia hushed her instantly, though the highwayman already knew they were inside. And as if she summoned him, he appeared at the door, on foot.

The smile beneath the mask riveted her, a flash of white teeth in the dark, and her arms tightened around her niece. She knew that smile, but she had never expected to see it like this, playful but with a threatening edge. What was he doing? She clicked her teeth to resist calling him out—saying his name, revealing his identity, needing to protect him—even though her mind couldn't wrap around seeing him here.

She pushed the younger woman behind her, and leveled a look at the man who accosted them, holding his gaze, wanting him to know she knew who he was.

"Well, well, lovely ladies indeed," he said, his voice intentionally rough to disguise it. "Please step outside."

Heart hammering, Julia shook her head so hard her hair fell loose, but she knew denial alone wouldn't send him away.

"All right," he said, lifting a lethal-looking pistol. "Just you, then. Bring her jewels with you."

Her hand went up to shield Constance instinctively, though she was certain Lucian wouldn't hurt her. "She's a debutante. She's only wearing pearls."

"Perfectly matched, if I recall. Bring them along, if you please."

"Don't do this. They're a family heirloom," Constance begged in a shaky voice.

"Perhaps the family'll pay a ransom for them, as well as for your lovely chaperone." He opened the door and held out his hand to Julia, while aiming the pistol at Constance. "The pearls, please."

"Julia!" Constance protested.

Where was their coachman? Their driver? Why did they have no protection? At the same time, she didn't want one of them to come around and shoot him. She couldn't watch Lucian die.

"Please, don't do this," Julia pleaded.

"I'd have you come with me. Now, if you please. And bring the pearls. I'll let the girl go."

Before she knew what was happening, Constance was pressing the pearls into her hand and practically shoving her out the door and into Lucian's arms.

"What are you doing?" Julia gasped against his jacket, the same he'd been wearing at the ball.

Not acknowledging her question, he didn't answer. Instead, he pulled the pearls from her hand then swept her into his arms and strode across the uneven ground to his restless horse. He lifted her onto the horse's back with more ease than she thought possible and followed her up, shoving her skirts aside. He wrapped an arm around her waist, his hand pressed against her stomach over her corset, pinning her to the breadth of his chest. He whirled his cape to shield her from the night air, pulled her back against him, and with a "hiya!" to the horse, galloped from the carriage.

Julia's mind spun, along with her stomach, as the horse raced along, Lucian holding her steady in the saddle. How had he come to this? Holding up carriages on the road? Robbing women? Was this why he hadn't come to her at Angelica's house? So many questions, and she could address none of them as the horse raced along.

She didn't know how long they rode or how far, before he turned the horse down a path. Once she adjusted her far-distant gaze to the cadence of the horse's gait, she saw they headed toward a darkened manor house.

He swerved from the house, and the horse gave another burst of speed before slowing. Lucian's chuckle reverberated in his chest, and the muscles of his arms tensed as he reined in the horse. A man melted from the shadow of a stable door, startling a shriek from Julia. The man took the horse's reins, and Julia shrank in Lucian's arms before she realized the groom waited to care for the horse.

Lucian swung out of the saddle and reached for her. When she didn't move right away, he closed his hands around her waist and lifted her down. He let her slide along his body, her skirt catching between them so that her stockinged legs brushed along his thighs.

Her body, numb from the shocking events of the evening, came alive. She hadn't been touched in months, and hadn't realized how she'd missed it. Now, the excitement of being kidnapped caught up, the blood rushing through her body and settling in every point of contact between them. Her nipples tightened, and her sex softened. She tightened her hands on his upper arms when he lowered her to her feet, and she looked up into his eyes, pale behind the mask. Something shifted in them, the mischief darkening to something else.

Then he set her away from him, turned her toward the house, and urged her ahead along the path. Vines grew up the brick walls, the bushes in front were unkempt, the rose bushes leggy and sparse, adding to an air of neglect. When she hesitated, he reached past her to open the heavy door, twice as tall as she was, dragging the bottom against the stone floor. He urged her through with his hand at the small of her back.

The foyer was dark, lit only from the moonlight glowing through large windows above.

"Lucian?" she asked shakily, turning toward him.

He went completely still before pivoting. "You knew?"

"Why are you doing this?" Despite herself, she shrank back as he advanced.

He sighed and shoved his mask up to his forehead. "I didn't want to frighten you, but I needed to send a message."

"A message? To whom?"

"I know how Joseph has been treating you. I wanted to get you away, but I didn't know how."

"So you kidnapped me? Terrified my niece? Brought me to a strange house?" Her voice rose with each question, even as a thrill raced through her blood.

He blew out a frustrated breath and moved to the entryway table where he lit a candelabra. When he turned toward her, casting flickering shadows, she jumped a foot to see a woman in the doorway, wearing a sleep-cap and robe, blinking.

"Master Lucian?"

"Go back to bed, Mrs. Tully," he said, not taking his gaze from Julia.

"You have a guest."

"I'll take care of her."

"Sir. It isn't proper."

He chuckled. "Go back to bed," he said again, tugging off his leather gloves and tossing them onto the table beside the candelabra.

After a moment, the older woman nodded and shuffled off.

"What are you going to do with me? Hold me for ransom? Angelica will never pay it. You should have kidnapped Constance. Though I'm glad you didn't."

He gave a crooked smile and stepped closer. "I didn't want her."

"I doubt you risked your life for only a string of pearls."

"You would be right." He held a hand out to her. "I came for you."

Julia stared at his hand, processing his words. "I don't understand."

"I have missed you. But I knew as long as you were in mourning, I couldn't take action. I didn't have the resources to look after you. I couldn't take you away from that house. But now I have the means to take care of you."

She shook her head. "I don't—you've been a highwayman? You've built your fortune that way?"

He chuckled. "Fortune, I wouldn't say. But a life better than you have now? That I can offer you."

She frowned, pressing her lips together. "But why?"

He took both her hands in his, and then folded them against his chest. "I love you. I've always loved you."

She took a step back, hands lifted. "You can't. I was Neville's wife."

"And the reason I never married was because there is no woman like you." He lifted his hand to her face. "Neville was the luckiest man I knew."

She didn't understand what he was saying. All those years where the three of them had attended dinners and parties, and he'd been in love with her? Knowing she went home with Neville and shared his bed? She and Neville had been a love match, and enjoyed each other, never making a secret of it. And Lucian had been in love with her, watching her go home with his best friend? "I don't know what to say. You—you left me behind."

"I didn't wish to. I wanted to sweep you away from the moment I knew you were moving in with Angelica. But I had nothing to offer you."

"So you turned to the life of a highwayman?"

"I had gambling debts. I lost not only Neville and you, but my home, everything."

"And you risk it all now?"

"More than you know." He touched her cheek, stroking his thumb across the rise.

His breath feathered across her lips. She caught her own breath at the intimacy and lifted her face a fraction. She jolted at the contact of his soft lower lip against hers.

He made a soft sound then curved his hand around the back of her head and angled his mouth over hers.

Unable to believe this was real, she trembled in his arms. Her body, dormant from months of grief and loneliness, blossomed to life. His fingers in her hair, his lips soft, the rasp of his stubble against her skin. The scent of him, musky and masculine with the hint of the night air. She moved closer, her hands on the sleeves of his coat to keep her balance as her head spun.

Lucian was kissing her. Lucian of the playful nature and the irresponsibility. Lucian of the laughing eyes and the quick smile. Lucian, whom every debutante flirted with before she found out he had no fortune. And he loved her.

His hand drifted down her back, stroking along her spine through the borrowed dress. She leaned into him, into the strength of his chest as his lips played over hers, as his tongue parted her lips, awakening a hunger she thought she'd buried forever.

She slid her hands inside his coat, down the row of buttons on his crisp white dress shirt, the one he'd worn to the ball, the one he'd danced in with Constance. He hadn't asked her to dance. Why? She wondered what it would be like to be twirled around the floor in his arms, to look into his eyes as they danced around the floor.

Wordlessly, he asked her to a more intimate dance now. His fingers pressed at the small of her back, and through the layers of her skirts, she felt the urgency of his cock. A flood of heat swept through her, laying waste to her good sense, and she leaned into him.

He made a sound deep in his throat—surprise or approval, she didn't know. But then he swept his hand behind her and lifted her into his arms. Startled, she wrapped hers around his neck. "Lucian?"

He didn't respond, instead striding toward the stairs and carrying her up.

Each step made her fingers tighten. She could stop this with a word, she was certain. She knew him—he was honorable, and he said he loved her.

But she couldn't find the word—or the will—to make him stop.

He continued through a doorway and closed the door behind them.

She presumed it was a bedroom, but the space was so dark so she couldn't be sure. He set her on her feet with her back to him and slid his hands from her shoulders down her bare arms. He pushed her gloves downward to caress her skin, his touch light as he stroked her forearms. She started to turn to face him, but he stopped her, bracing his legs on either side of her, moving closer so that his breath was hot against her neck, but other than his fingertips on her arms, he didn't touch her.

He tugged the gloves free one at a time and tossed them aside, and then glided his touch up to the gown's short sleeves, pulling them down to bare her shoulders.

Lucian touched his lips to the tender skin of her shoulder, and she caught her breath, swaying at the power of the simple yet intimate caress. Her entire being centered on the way he was touching her, on the anticipation of what was to come.

But he was in no hurry. He ran his lips across the cap of her shoulder, then repeated the caress on her other arm. Every inch of her skin anticipated his touch.

He loosened her hair so it tumbled around her, cool and heavy. He swept aside the length and kissed the side of her throat, nipped the tip of her ear.

Her breasts swelled in her bodice, needing his hands, which remained on her arms. She could feel a tremor in his touch, a hitch in his breathing that told her he was as affected as she.

Finally, he moved his hand to the back of her neck, stroking downward, his arm between their bodies, until he reached the laces of her gown.

She caught her breath when he began to tug. She tried not to think about the ease with which he loosened them, only about the way his fingertips stroked her skin as he bared it.

The borrowed dress sagged from her body then dropped to the floor, and he lifted her off her feet again, only to set her down outside of the circle of pooled fabric, this time facing him. Her eyes had become accustomed to the dark, and moonlight filtered in through a large window, making the loathed lavender dress and the cream-colored bedding glow.

He curved his hand around her jaw, angling her head up for another kiss, at the same time tucking her hair back over her shoulder, out of his way as he ran his hand down the slope of her breast still covered by her corset. She gasped into his mouth as the heat of his hand permeated the thin fabric, and she pushed her breast into his touch. He took his time, concentrating on her mouth, kissing, nipping, stroking her lower lip with his tongue before diving deeper. Only then, when his mouth was sealed against hers, did he take her nipple in his fingers and pluck gently.

Her entire body sagged as heat raced between her legs, swelling the flesh there until she was almost reduced to begging for his touch to ease the ache.

Then he broke the kiss and bent his head, nuzzling aside the fabric of her corset and chemise to take the tip of her breast into his mouth, hot and deep, sucking and drawing and—

A climax swept over her, making her cry out as her body bowed over his arm, as her fingers dug into his hair, holding his head to her, not willing to release him, to end the sensation.

He broke her hold to look up at her, eyes bright. "Was that—?"

She nodded, her head flopping on her neck since her muscles had turned to water.

He grinned and straightened, lifting her once more and carrying her toward the bed.

"Will you always be carrying me about to get me where you want me?" she demanded.

He rose over her on the mattress. "Perhaps."

"You could simply ask. I might say yes."

His nostrils flared, and he opened his mouth, like he was going to ask her something, but then he lowered his mouth to hers.

This time, his kiss was decidedly more passionate—his tongue sweeping into her mouth, his hands bracing him over her. His knees trapped her chemise, pinning her legs to the bed. She wriggled beneath him, trying to free himself, her struggle seeming to excite him for his breathing came faster, hotter, harder.

"Lucian." She reached between them and tried to pull the fabric free before he understood.

He rolled to the side and pushed the skirt to her hips, his fingers stroking along the skin he bared.

At the caress, her entire body sparked, and she lifted her body toward him.

Again, he pulled her underneath him, his breeches rasping against her inner thighs. Wondering why she was undressed and he wasn't, she slid one leg along the outside of his. He broke the kiss to trail his lips down her jaw, down her throat, over the curve of her breast where it swelled above her corset.

She bowed off the bed, urging his mouth lower, needing the heat of his mouth.

He turned his head to her other breast, then nudged

aside the fabric to pull her nipple into his mouth. He stroked his tongue against it before drawing it deep.

Her entire body tightened. That she was so eager after her first climax shocked her. She opened her legs and rubbed her sex against his cock, hard in his breeches, needing to ease the ache, needing him inside her.

Her corset made breathing difficult. She twisted, reaching for the laces.

Again, he sensed her need and flipped her over. She heard a rasp, and the garment fell loose. When she turned over, she saw Lucian tossing a knife onto the table beside the bed. She gave a soft whimper of longing as he grabbed the corset and tossed it across the room, the hooks clattering against the window.

Then he turned and ripped the chemise from her torso. He rocked back on his heels to look and smoothed his palm down the center of her body, from throat to sex, stroking his fingers through the curls to find her, slick and ready. Gliding his fingers over her wet petals, he circled the nub of pleasure before dipping inside her, one finger sliding deep, and then a second.

He watched her face, and she tried to hold his gaze, until she couldn't deal with the intimacy and let her lids slide closed, giving herself over to the sensations as his rough fingers hooked inside her.

Still, the sensation wasn't enough. She wanted him inside her. Lazily, she glanced at his crotch and reached for the buttons of his breeches.

But he pushed her hand away.

"Lucian."

"Take what I have to give you, Julia," he said, and slid down her body, following the same path his palm had taken, until he spread her thighs, his thumbs parting the lips of her sex, and he lowered his mouth.

The flick of his tongue against that hard little pearl at the top of her sex shot a sizzling sensation through her, and she tried to slam her thighs together, the pleasure stunning and terrifying. "Lucian!"

"Let me. Julia. Let me give you this." He held her thighs open, and let his breath blow warm against her inner thighs, then over her damp curls. Her stomach tightened, her sex flooded with desire, and she tilted her hips in invitation.

Again, he touched his tongue to her. She closed her fingers over his shoulders, intent on pushing him away, but when he continued the caress, her fingers found their way into his hair, holding him to her. His tongue alternately lapped and pressed against her, until she was lifting off the bed against him, grinding her hips into his mouth.

The climax rocked through her body, and the next thing she knew, he'd stripped off his shirt, peeled down his pants, and pressed his cock against her opening. He was hard, hot, and heavy as he eased forward, his body shaking.

She understood what that meant and hooked her legs around his naked hips, his firm buttocks, and brought him inside.

Both of them gasped, she at the pinch as he stretched her, as he filled her, as his groin pressed into her sex. He was so deep inside her, she arched her back, as if that could give him more room. His breathing was heavy as he braced himself above and looked down at her.

And then he began to move, the drag of his cock inside her sparking arousal all over again, the wet sound of him leaving her body only to return with more force, the collision of his hips with her swollen flesh. She tightened her legs around him, beneath his buttocks, and slid her hands from shoulders to thigh, following the play of muscles, settling her touch over the bunch and thrust of his ass.

He took her face in one hand and guided her to him, kissing her for a long moment. "I've wanted to be inside you since I first met you," he murmured, before rising to drive into her again and again, each push harder, rocking her on the mattress.

His words sent a sense of power through her, and she pushed at his shoulder until he understood and rolled onto his back, carrying her with him, almost sliding free, grabbing her ass just in time to anchor himself. She adjusted her hips as she straddled his, bringing him deep again. His nostrils flared as he stroked her breasts, her waist, her hips and thighs. She allowed the caresses before she began to move, her thighs protesting the motion she hadn't indulged in for too long, but the wonder on Lucian's face was worth the sting.

Each thrust made him tense, and he gripped her hips, rising to meet her, until they lost the rhythm in their desperation for completion. She rolled her hips once more, and he shouted and stilled beneath her, so she felt his seed pumping into her with a violence she couldn't have predicted.

Moments later, he sat up, his body still pulsing, and captured her nipple in his mouth, pulling on it as he slid his hand between her thighs to caress her center of pleasure. After two climaxes, she was surprised to respond, her whole body becoming tight, focused, until he stroked one thumb upward, sending her tumbling into another vortex of sensation.

She slid off of him and tumbled to the mattress beside him. He stared at the ceiling for a moment as he struggled for breath.

"I can't believe I finally have you in my bed." He turned his head toward her, and his smile flashed in the moonlight. "Now that I have you here, I may never let you out."

Dreamily, she reached across the bed, across the rumpled sheets and stroked his skin, slick with sweat. "Lucian, I can't stay."

He rolled onto his elbow and looked downward. "You don't understand, Julia. I mean to marry you. Will you have me?"

Her brain whirled. He loved her, he wanted her, he wanted to marry her? How was a woman to insert reason when a man literally swept her off of her feet? But she had to try. "Lucian. I can't—you don't—we need time."

"We've had time. I can give you my heart. Will you take it, Julia? Will you take me? Body and soul?"

"And what about your nightly activities?" She waved toward the window. "What of them? You'd have me be the wife of a highwayman?"

He chuckled and drew her against him. "Oh, I have a very definite plan about that."

★ ★ ★

Six months later

"STAND AND DELIVER!"

From astride her own mount, Julia watched her dashing new husband approach the same carriage he'd removed her from. She tugged at her mask as he prodded her brother-in-law from the safety of the conveyance and onto the road, forcing him to kneel with his hands behind his head. Julia could hear his sniveling as he pled for his life.

Lucian ignored him and motioned the gun for the other occupants of the carriage to disembark. Not one of them her sister-in-law, Julia noted, not as shocked as she should be. Lucian swiftly divested the two women of their jewels, and he leveled his gun at Joseph's head once more, drawing back the hammer of the gun.

Joseph sobbed in earnest now, but Lucian was in no mood to show mercy. He swung the pistol against the side of the man's head so that he crumpled in the dirt. Then Lucian swung up onto his mount and motioned to her.

Together, they wheeled their horses in the other direction and galloped away, capes flowing behind.

Plunder

Delilah Night

"YE'RE KEEPING AN eye out for pirates?" Captain Marcus, her father's right-hand man and current captain of the *Maya*, leaned against the *Maya's* gunwale. A tic pulsed beside his good eye.

Brianna Northerly heard the comment from her honorary second father and felt her face redden with anger. But she pulled on the lessons she'd learned in that infernal finishing school she'd escaped and counted slowly to ten.

At school, Bree had been an outcast. While the other girls obsessed over finding a husband, Bree knew she was already promised to her great love, the ocean. Spending her formative years on the *Maya*, the crown jewel in her father's fleet of merchant ships, made her a sailor to her very core.

When Bree was rescued by her father's right-hand man Marcus from Mrs. Lingstrom's stifling tutelage days ago, she'd thought her dreams of returning to the sea were coming true. Instead, she was living out her worst nightmare.

Drawing a deep breath, she gave Marcus a sour look and gestured to the cumbersome dress swathing her body. "Watching for pirates is about all I can do in this get-up. I can't even climb to the crow's nest. I don't suppose you'd be willing to give me a pair of breeches—"

The grizzled sailor rolled his eyes at her seventh request for trousers that day. "Lass, yer father made it clear that ye're to be dressing and acting like a lady. I'll already catch hell for ye shearing off yer hair short as a boy's."

"It got in the way. Just like this blasted dress."

"No. Ye're a lady now. Act like it. God knows ye need all the practice ye can get to convince anyone of that fact."

"You're a traitorous piece of chum," she snapped waspishly. "You're following my father's orders like a brainless dog on a leash, content to lick your own balls rather than show your spine."

Marcus laughed. "Three years at a school to learn a girl's manners and ye've still got a sailor's mouth." He clapped her on the back and moved on.

Clenching her jaw, she turned back to the water and thought, *Damned pirates.*

After her mother died in childbirth, Bree had grown up a ship's brat. By sixteen, she'd been certain it was only a matter of time until her father made her an officer, and eventually, captain of the *Maya*.

Then the pirates came. The ship had been attacked near Anguilla. They hadn't been boarded, but the threat had been close enough. Still, the damage had been done.

Someone—and wouldn't she like to know who—convinced Papa that *she* was the greatest plunder the ship had to offer. He'd begun spouting nonsense about him managing ships from the land and her making a "proper marriage."

Three years she'd suffered at boarding school in America.

Embroidery. Mending sails or the occasional piece of clothing was worthy of her time, but stitching decorative roses on pieces of silk?

Penmanship. She could read and write just fine, but the teacher wanted her to draw letters so precious and curlicued they were near illegible.

She'd sent Papa countless letters, begging to come home. *He finally sends Marcus to fetch me, only to tell me I'm to be married to the owner of a sugar plantation? A landlubber!*

No matter. She'd figure out how to sail these sorry straits, and still come out without so much as a rigging out of place—or a ring on her finger. Somehow.

Late that afternoon Brianna was watching clouds form on the horizon. They would need all hands on deck if a storm blew in. Her hands were better than most when to the task was tying ropes in the rain.

Bree was trying to persuade Marcus to let her take charge of the rigging when a cry rang out from above.

"Pirates! Off the port bow!"

Instinctively, Bree pulled up her skirts and made to climb the rigging when an arm came about her waist.

A sailor dragged her below decks and pushed her into the nearest cabin. "Stay in there, miss. Captain's orders."

The door slammed shut, and she heard him dash away. "The hell I will." Bree spied a chest and helped herself to a shirt and breeches, discarding the hated gown. A length of rope served as a makeshift belt. Keeping her boots was one of the few concessions she'd nagged out of Marcus. Snatching a cutlass from where it hung on the wall, Brianna charged back up to the deck.

The sight of the ship nearing the port bow sent chills up her spine. A three-masted, black pirate ship with blood-red trim and a silver flag was gaining on the *Maya*. It was the *Ghost*. A cannonball ripped through the air and crashed into the water. A warning shot. If they didn't surrender, the next would hit the *Maya*.

Looking around, Bree saw the foresail was unmanned. One corner had come undone and flapped uselessly. She dashed over to the ratlines and nimbly climbed to the crossbar. Her muscles screamed as she secured the rigging. Bree prayed for a wind that would allow the *Maya* to escape, but it was no use. They couldn't outrun the *Ghost*, and their cannons weren't powerful enough to span the distance. Soon enough her fears were proven true. They'd been maneuvered into a cay with no way to escape. Time to surrender or die.

Marcus looked as if he'd aged a decade in the past hour. His voice quavered as he gave the orders every sailor dreaded. "Lower the flag. Put down your weapons. Prepare to be boarded."

The sailor to Bree's left threw down his knife in disgust. He looked at Bree. "They say, if you see the

Ghost, you're about to become one. You should ask the captain to slit your throat. They're not letting *you* go, no matter what they do to the lot of us."

"I'd rather die defending the ship than be a coward," she spat. She held her cutlass ready, refusing to drop it. Brianna wasn't about to submit to a pirate any more than she was willing to submit to the owner of a sugar plantation. *Her* choice, not someone else's.

Even so, she shuddered at the sound of the pirate longboat bump the *Maya*. The boarding ladder scraped the hull as pirates climbed. All too soon men were swarming the ship. Their leader was tall, with the kind of tanned skin that spoke of a life at sea, and the muscles of a man unafraid to work alongside his crew. Bree was surprised to see his face was clean-shaven—an odd affectation—and cursed herself for noticing his full, sensual lips.

The pirate captain marched up the line of the *Maya*'s sailors, coldly assessing each man. Other pirates walked behind him, gathering weapons and yelling orders at the forfeited crew. Marcus was surrounded and forced below decks.

Seeing the pirate stride closer made Brianna clutch her cutlass. No man here might have the balls to attack the pirates, but she did.

His glance cut to her sword. "Put it down, lad. Don't think to try me."

Defiantly, she stepped out of line and faced him.

He raised an eyebrow at the gentle curve of her breasts beneath her shirt.

His distraction presented the perfect opportunity. She lunged. Bree grinned fiercely as she scored first blood, a slice across his side, but her victory was short-lived.

With quick moves, he parried, hooked her weapon with his, and tossed it away, disarming her. In the space between one heartbeat and the next, she found herself face down on the deck with the pirate captain's boot planted firmly on her back. Humiliation heated her cheeks.

This would never have happened if Papa hadn't sent me away. Fighting had been yet another useful skill she'd abandoned in favor of nonsense like bossing around servants. Maids were bigger crybabies than seasick boys on their first sail.

"This girl has more courage than the rest of you scum put together. At least she tried to kill me," he said derisively.

The boot was removed, and the pirate captain hauled her to her feet.

She immediately cocked a fist.

"Quite the spitfire, aren't you?" The captain ducked her swing and grabbed her waist. The world spun as he lifted her in the air and tossed her over his shoulder like a sack of flour.

Her blood boiled. "Go to hell!" She beat at his back as he carried her to the quarterdeck. Abruptly, he bent and set her on her feet with her back to the railing.

The pirate imprisoned her hands in one of his own. "I have a proposition, minx. You've given me more amusement in the past five minutes than I've had in a long time. Amuse me tonight, and I won't kill your crewmates. Perhaps, you'll even please me so well I'll let you keep your ship."

The roar in her ears wasn't the ocean. "What?"

His bright blue eyes glittered with amusement. "Don't disappoint me now. Is the idea of my bed so repulsive that you'd rather lose your ship?"

Her heart hammering, Bree swallowed and lifted her chin. "How do I know you'll honor the bargain?" *My body is to be a bargaining chip, no matter what. Better to use it for the* Maya *than submit to whomever Papa chose.*

He gave her a feral smile. "You don't."

She was insulted to feel her nipples sharpen in response. "Do I have your word none of the crew is to be harmed until tomorrow morning?" *Maybe the landlubber won't want a bride who's already been tumbled...*

"That depends on the persuasion of your lips right now. Kiss me." He released her hands and straightened, waiting.

Her skin was alive with the kind of anticipation she experienced in those moments before a squall blew in. *My choice.* Heat kindled between her legs. Brianna took a fistful of the pirate's shirt. She yanked to bring his mouth to hers and bit his lower lip before lightly sucking on it. His arms banded about her, and their lips fused. His tongue plundered her mouth, and she matched every thrust and parry.

When they broke for air, he chuckled. "Direct hit. Very well, decisions can wait until the morning."

Clasping her hand, he led her to his men. "Take her back to the ship and stow her in my cabin. No one touches her but me."

One kiss, and he's robbed me of my sea legs. Bree was silent as she was rowed back to the *Ghost* and led to his cabin.

One of his men pointed at the bed. "Wait there." The pirate leaned against the captain's desk.

His action was clear—he was not leaving her alone. She considered engaging the pirate in conversation, but the way he was playing with a knife kept her meek. Desire ebbed, and fear rose the longer she waited.

When the pirate captain finally opened the door, she felt a mix of relief and fear. He jerked his head, and her jailer left. He locked his cutlass and knives into a trunk and smirked at Brianna's obvious disappointment. She watched as he shrugged out of his coat, tossing it onto his table. He tugged a tie from his hair. Black curls fell about his shoulders. She clenched her fists, resisting the urge to touch them.

The pirate looked her over stem-to-stern before he spoke. "Your father owns the *Maya*."

"What of it?" She jutted her chin.

"You're unmarried."

"So?"

He closed the distance between them and traced a path from her collarbone to the dirty rope holding up her breeches. "Virgin?"

Narrowing her gaze, she swallowed. He had the rope in his hands. Every horrible lecture she'd received about wifely duties and being brave in the face of a *manhood* flooded her mind.

She pushed them aside, remembering the feel of his mouth upon hers. Lifting her chin, she responded, "Not after tonight."

He laughed. "What am I to call you, minx?"

"Brianna. Bree. And you? What shall I call you? Blackguard? Criminal?"

He answered her with a kiss. A seductive kiss. His mouth was surprisingly gentle, and her lips opened for him. Unable to resist, she slid her arms around his neck, pulling him closer. His hands stroked down her back, cupping her bottom. An eddy of heat formed in Brianna's lower stomach.

"William," he murmured. He nuzzled her neck, and a shiver ran down her back. "My name is William."

Bree began to melt like the wax beneath a flame. *No! You're not a simpering schoolgirl.* She shoved him away. "What game is this? You proposition me, hold me hostage in your quarters, and then kiss me like a lovestruck cabin boy?"

Despite her resistance, he tightened his embrace. His voice rumbled against her skin as he nibbled his way up her neck. "Any wench can open her legs and ignore a man pumping above her. That's a hollow victory. I want your complete surrender. When I take you, you'll know who it is inside you." He whispered in her ear, "You'll want me there."

At his words, an unfamiliar current formed within her, and she shivered. Her tongue darted out to trace over suddenly dry lips. She tasted the familiar tang of sea air, ocean spray, and *him*.

"A few kisses and you think it's clear skies ahead?" Her retort lacked heat.

William reached out and cupped a breast. His thumb brushed a mutinous nipple thrusting against the cotton of her stolen shirt. Brianna gasped as his finger moved back and forth, teasing it. Her other nipple ached, craving the same treatment.

His narrowed gaze studied her expression. "Is there something you want?"

Brianna clenched her jaw and shook her head.

His thumb and forefinger squeezed and lightly tugged at the nipple. The ache in her other breast became an insistent throbbing. *Who knew you could do so much by* not *doing something?* "Fine!" she spat as her fingers tightened into her palms. "Touch the other breast, just like that."

"Now, was it so hard to admit you want more?"

Her hand itched to slap that arrogant look off his face. She weighed the momentary satisfaction the action would give her against the effect his hands were now having on both her breasts and found it wanting. "I hate you."

He laughed. "Of course you do." His mouth possessed hers as he tugged her shirt free from her breeches.

Bree greedily kissed him back, hands fisting in his shirt to keep from mimicking his movements. What would his skin feel like? Taste like? When his hands slid under her shirt to touch her breasts without any barrier, she moaned.

"What do you want me to do, Bree? Send you back to your ship? Or will you ask me to remove your shirt? Your breeches?"

"I'm perfectly capable of removing my own shirt—and yours—if I wanted to." She meant the words to be tart, but a tremble underscored them.

William's fingers pinched her nipples. A flash of pain caused her to gasp, but was quickly followed by a rush of wanton pleasure. A sensation, like the heady swell of a wave, broke between her thighs. As desire won, she cursed and yanked off her shirt. She raised her chin, daring him to laugh.

Had his eyes always been that shade of dark Caribbean blue? Or were they like the ocean, always shifting depending on his mood? Did William look at every woman the way he now looked at her?

"You're beautiful."

The simplicity of the words undid Brianna. She pulled William's shirt free and upwards over his head. She'd seen many shirtless men over her years at sea, but he was the first that she was free to touch as she liked. Two dark nipples peeked out from the hair of his chest. A trail led to, and then disappeared into, his breeches. She felt some small satisfaction at the sight of the scratch on his side from where her cutlass had nicked his skin.

What do I do now?

She had enjoyed his touch on her nipples. Would a similar caress feel equally pleasurable for him? Nervously, she reached out and touched one. Hearing William groan at her touch gave Bree a swell of confidence. She had the wicked impulse to use her tongue instead, so leaning forward, she flicked his nipple with the tip of her tongue. He swore. Bree was invigorated by his reactions as she licked and suckled the sensitive skin. Her hands roamed the hard planes of his chest, enjoying the feel of his warm skin and wiry hair.

This would be far more comfortable if they weren't standing. Bree looked up at William. "The bed?"

"Yes, there is a bed. Very good. What would you like to do on it? Recite a sonnet?" He was a bit breathless.

Apparently, he wasn't giving her any quarter. She arched a brow. "At school, they didn't mention sonnets. Mrs. Lingstrom said something about closing your eyes and thinking of your duty." Teasing, she glanced from beneath the fringe of her lashes. "Would you like me to close my eyes and think of my ship while declaiming a specific sonnet?"

William picked her up and tossed her onto his bed. "I wonder what perversion causes me to find you more enticing with each insult you lob my way." He paused to remove her boots and then his own.

When William leaned over Bree, she pulled him down to her. The feel of his skin against hers was more intoxicating than grog. Her legs parted and his clothed thigh pressed against her center. The insistent pressure of his rod sent another wave of desire through her body.

William's mouth was everywhere. He possessed her lips. He nibbled and nipped at her neck. He feasted at her breasts. He pressed kisses against her arms, her stomach, and her face.

"Parlay, William," she gasped. "My breeches. Remove them. Touch me."

"No truce," he growled. "Make your choice. Are you mine?"

Brianna reached down and grasped him through the rough material of his breeches. "Why not say you're mine instead?"

"My ship, my woman." His gaze fierce and thrilling, he cupped her mound. "Wave the white flag, just for tonight."

My choice.

Brianna's hips moved. She needed his touch. "Remove my breeches and convince me to do so."

Within seconds, the rope was undone and the breeches flew across the room. He kissed her belly, moving slowly downward. As if they'd lain together a thousand times, her legs parted for him. He settled between her thighs.

"What are you—" The question became a moan as his tongue found her.

What began as an eddy had become a whirlpool. Desire spiraled out of control. She knew the only way out of a whirlpool was to oppose the pull and steer free. Only a fool stopped fighting the wheel. In that moment, Bree knew this man was capable of making her such a fool. "I surrender."

"Again!" He barked the order and dove back between her thighs, tongue sending her into a frenzy.

"I surrender! Oh God, I surrender! Just don't stop, William!"

Every inch of her body felt the pull of a powerful current moving to the spot his tongue worshipped. Bree took hold of his curls to tug him closer still as her hips bucked beneath his magical tongue. Everything was spinning faster and faster as she was pulled down into the vortex. Something broke free within her, and screaming his name, she let the maelstrom have her.

Breathing heavily, Bree felt the churning waters from which the whirlpool had sprung begin to calm. *The ceiling of his cabin has more stars than the night sky. Or maybe I'm just seeing things.*

It might have been seconds, minutes, or hours later, when she felt his weight settle above her. His breeches were gone. He was gloriously naked.

"Tell me again."

His eyes did change with his mood. Despite everything, she could see uncertainty there. Warmth spread inside her chest. "I surrender. My choice."

William reached down and stroked her. Bree's hips rocked against him as she felt a new storm brewing.

"Now, now, now," she chanted, unsure what she was asking for.

William's cock nudged where she was flooded with need. "Say you're mine, Bree."

"I'm yours, William."

Adrift in pleasure, she felt him enter her. She had been lied to. No pain bloomed as her maidenhead broke. Once he was fully within her, there was a sense of completeness, as if she'd placed the last piece of a puzzle.

William began to move. Brianna's hips found the rhythm and lifted to match him thrust for thrust. Her legs wrapped around his waist, greedy to pull him deeper, to keep him there. Their kisses grew more urgent as his thrusts sped. They were so absorbed in one another the ship could have capsized, and neither would have noticed.

William's body stiffened, and he growled her name as he came. Moments later, he settled on the bed next to her.

She was pleased his eyes were still a bit unfocused with pleasure. He was reaching for a blanket to pull over them both when she stopped him. "What are you doing?"

"Darling, clearly it's your nature to argue over everything, but it's a blanket. It's warm. You sleep under it."

"I didn't say I was ready to sleep." Bree plucked the blanket from his hand and tossed it to the floor. "I've yet to fully explore your territory."

A chuckle escaped. "I suppose I can close my eyes and think of my duty to cartography."

Bree's hand had been trailing through his chest hair. At his comment, she grabbed a fistful and tugged.

"Vicious little vixen."

"Damned pirate. Turn over."

"Aye aye, wench."

All mine.

Her hands roamed his body. William tensed at her touch on his left shoulder. Her touch gentled and massaged the knot there. When he was again quiet, she pressed a kiss to the spot and continued her journey. Freckles were scattered over his back, and she made note of their constellation. He was ticklish behind his right knee. With her fingertips, she traced the corded muscles of his calves.

"Where did you get this?" An odd scar marred the perfection of his buttocks.

"Slight disagreement with a shark."

She dug her nails into the cheek.

William sighed deeply. "Slight disagreement with a fishing hook. Rum was involved."

Bree laughed with delight. "Turn over, and let me see what other wounds have been inflicted upon your body. I wish to catalog them all."

He turned onto his back. "What of the wound *you* gave me, minx?"

"A memory I shall always cherish." Her tone was tart, but her gaze softened as she made a study of his form.

His manhood had stood at half-mast when he first turned, but beneath her eager gaze, he grew fully erect. Bree felt an answering tug within her body. She tapped his thighs, and they parted, allowing her to kneel between them.

Slowly, she traced the trail of hair from his chest downward, stopping just short of touching him. Bree's nails scratched a path from knees to hips. Each time she approached his manhood, she saw William's eyes become a storm that built with each denied opportunity.

Enjoying the rush of power, Bree moved to her

hands and knees. Pressing her hands to the mattress, she leaned forward to take his cock between her breasts. She rocked her body back and forth.

His hands banded about her wrists. "Don't stop."

She immediately stopped and smirked, saying nothing.

"You'd try the patience of a saint." His head fell back, and his hands released her.

Bree shifted her body lower. She cupped the heavy sack between his thighs and let the anticipation grow.

"Brianna."

The needy way he said her name made her breasts ache for his touch. She took him in her hand. Bree had never felt anything that was both so hard and so soft all at once. Her hand slid up and down. Moving closer, she licked the head of his penis as her hand attended to the shaft.

"Suck me, minx." A pleading tone sounded beneath the growl. His hands were fisted in the bed sheets to keep from grabbing her again.

Her tongue circled the head several times before she took him into her mouth. Brianna let herself feel the motion of the ship and let her movements be guided by the gentle bobbing. As William's groans increased, an ache pulsed in her quim. She suckled him with increasing enthusiasm.

"I'm close, lass. Decide if you're going to finish there or climb aboard."

Smiling, Brianna lifted her head. "Prepare to be boarded."

He chuckled. "Come here, darling."

Bree climbed astride his body and poised herself above his cock. "Surrender?"

"No." He gave her a cocky smile. "Now what?"

"To the lowest hells with you," she spat and impaled herself upon him.

His thumb found her clit and stroked her. Her hips rocked back and forth, greedy for more. She took her breasts into her hands and teased her nipples as he had. He groaned beneath her, urging her on.

"I can't take much more, Bree. Come for me, love!"

Brianna welcomed the hurricane they'd created. Lightning flew through her body. Her blood was the thunder booming in her ears. Wave after wave of pleasure broke over her. And the word *love* capsized her heart.

Afterward, he held her the way a drowning man would cling to driftwood—as if she spelled his salvation. Brianna allowed herself the fantasy of being William's lass as she drifted off to sleep, having completely forgotten why she was there.

I'd be happy if I were his.

Bree awoke to an obscenely bright morning. She frowned at finding herself alone and sat up. One of her dresses from the *Maya* lay draped over the desk. The message was clear—get dressed. A cold shiver passed through her body. She did so and opened the door of the cabin.

Marcus was waiting. "I'm to take ye back to the *Maya*."

Her gaze flicked past her friend. "But what about—"

"Lass, he says we can have our lives, our ship, and our cargo," he said gruffly with a shrug. "What more do you want?"

The question was like a slap across the face. The girlish dreams that had formed in the hours after sex evaporated.

As she followed Marcus down the ladder to the longboat, she could feel her temper rising. They rowed away, and she spotted William at the helm of the *Ghost*, arms crossed over his chest. She couldn't discern his expression, but she imagined one of smug satisfaction at her eager surrender.

Damned pirate.

"You bastard! You think you can send me away like this? Coward!" Curses rained from her lip as Marcus implored her to hush. As the distance between the rowboat and the *Ghost* grew, she continued to berate the pirates whose rowing conveyed them back to the *Maya*. "And you tell him I said so!" she spat as she climbed aboard her vessel.

Her last days at sea were spent stewing and plotting in her cabin.

Papa met her and Marcus at the docks. He would escort her to Monsieur Martine's plantation, where the marriage papers would be signed with Marcus as a witness. Papa seemed pleased by Bree's docile appearance. Marcus kept a narrowed gaze on her movements.

Rough waters raged beneath her calm surface. They could force her to come here. They could even order her to marry Martine. But they couldn't make *him* want to marry *her*. Sharing the lurid story of her night as a pirate's whore should end this marriage before it began. She'd be back on the *Maya* by nightfall, and she *would* convince her father to drop this fantasy of her spending her days as a lady.

Brianna wasn't sure who she hated more—William for discarding her so easily, or herself for her body's response to the memory of her pirate. Those full sensual lips. His broad shoulders. His eyes. As they waited in the landlubber's parlor, she let memories of that night wash over her.

"Monsieur Martine."

Bree froze as he entered the room. She stood as still as a statue when Martine took her hand and raised it for a kiss. Then fury overtook shock, and she slapped him as hard as she could.

"Brianna!" Papa gasped.

Marcus grabbed Papa's arm and began whispering urgently to his oldest friend in a low voice.

William laughed. "I had a feeling that would be your reaction. Do you want an explanation?"

Biting back a screech, she picked up a vase from a nearby table and hurled it at the wall.

"Was that a yes or a no?"

"Tell me," she growled. She took inventory of every other breakable within reach should the impulse strike again.

William spun the tale of a sailor who ran away and became a pirate. Who saved every last share of booty until he could afford his own ship, and later this island with its defunct sugar plantation.

"The problem with producing rum is that everyone wants to take it. Steal your product, pillage your land, and attack your people. Damned pirates." At this, he winked at Brianna, who glared in response. "What better way to scare off pirates but to invent a scarier pirate?"

The island was full of other former pirates who wanted to retire and raise families. They worked the plantation, made the rum, and patrolled the waters. William encouraged his men to travel to other islands and spin tales of the *Ghost* and the vicious pirates aboard her. He backed it up by capturing or killing pirates and slavers, granting a safe home to those who wanted one.

"The problem with being a rum producer is that I have to be social. Other plantation owners, merchants, and so forth. I need a wife. Someone who could put on the proper manners when necessary, you see? But all I met were these soft girls with no spine. Nothing at all like you."

She gave him a blistering glare. He'd played her for a fool. "I aim to geld you."

"Of course, you will. Uncle Marcus told me he thought we'd suit. I saw him in a tavern on Barbados about six months ago and told him of my troubles. He knew your pa wanted to marry you off, but that you'd suit a gentleman about as well as a lady suits me."

"Uncle Marcus?" Bree and her father spoke as one.

"I'm the family embarrassment, what with my piracy and all," William said it with no small amount of pride.

"For ye to steal her away and ruin her virtue wasn't part of the plan," Marcus spat. "That was dishonorable."

William shrugged. "Ma would tell you pirates have no honor. Besides, a spitfire like you described required a special sort of courting. Brianna's virtue is her own business." He turned to Bree and took her hands in his own. "You once asked me what you should call me." His gaze locked with hers. "Why not husband?"

Somewhat pacified by William's declaration of her right to bodily autonomy, Brianna gave him a wicked grin. "That depends. Will you give me a wedding present?"

His gaze narrowed in suspicion. "Name your plunder, minx."

She bit his lower lip before kissing him in earnest. "The *Ghost*. I'll call you husband. You'll call me *Captain*."

The Heat

Mia Hopkins

A WINTER STORM hammered the coast for three days straight. Sheets of rain bore down on the lone house on the hill. Waterfalls raced down the sharp slant of the saltbox roof. By Friday evening, Helen had grown so numb to the sound of the rain that she almost didn't hear the knock at the door.

She put down the speech she was writing for her next suffragette meeting. When she looked out the window, she saw a tall stranger.

Wrapping her wool shawl around her shoulders, she opened the door a crack. Chilled air and the tattoo of raindrops rushed into the room. "Can I help you?"

The stranger took off his hat, dumping water on her threshold. "Missus." His voice was deep. "I'm sorry to bother you. I'm looking for a place to stay for the night."

She looked up at him. His overcoat was soaked and his shoes—fancy city shoes—were caked with mud. In the shadows, all she could see of his face was his heavy jaw, shaded in reddish-blond stubble.

"This isn't a boarding house. Half Moon Bay is six

miles up the road. Mabel in town probably has something better suited for a gentleman." She began to close the door.

The stranger lifted his hand and held it open. "Missus." His voice was weary at the edges. "I was on my way home to San Francisco. This rain has done a number on the roads. My car got stuck in the mud. I've been trying to get free for the past two hours. I'm played out. Please. I'd be happy to pay. Name your price."

Helen frowned. "Where did you get stuck?"

"Bend in the road, just at the foot of your driveway."

"That's been a problem for years. I've asked the mayor—multiple times—to send a road crew down to fix that berm. But nothing has happened." She studied the stranger up and down, slowly taking him in. "What's your name?"

"James O'Connor."

"Keep your money. I expect you need some dry clothes and a hot meal in you, Mr. O'Connor?"

"I do."

His slow, handsome smile made Helen blink.

"I'm much obliged, Missus...?"

"Baker." She opened the door. "Come in out of the cold."

As the stranger went upstairs to change, Helen flipped a ham steak in the cast iron skillet, and it sizzled in the hot fat. She opened a jar of pickled beans and poured a glass of milk. By the time the stranger came into the kitchen, a hot meal waited on the table.

"Did the clothes fit?" she asked.

"Yes. Thank you, missus."

"Have your supper before it gets cold."

As he ate, Helen worked on her speech and watched him out of the corner of her eye. The stranger was as handsome as a film star. Besides his sharp jaw, he had a high forehead, a fine straight nose, and heavy-lidded eyes of icy blue. His short reddish-blond hair was disheveled. Peter's shirt and trousers hung on his rangy frame, but instead of looking gangly, O'Connor looked lithe and strong.

O'Connor must have been observing her as closely as she was observing him. When he spoke up, she startled at her work. She left a messy blob of ink on the paper.

"If you don't mind my asking," he said, looking at her face, "how did your husband pass away?"

"How did you know he passed away?"

"If he were here, I'd be dealing with him. If he were away, you wouldn't have let me in."

"Clever." She put down her pen. "My husband was in the war. France. He survived. He came home to me. Then influenza took him down three months later."

"How long ago was that?"

"Two years come November. He was twenty-five." She took a deep breath and let it out slowly. She felt only a dull echo of anger where her heart used to be. Rain hammered pitilessly at the roof.

"Survived the Kaiser. Taken down by *la grippe*. Hardly seems fair."

"Tell it to God." She looked into his pale blue eyes.

"I was honest with you. Now be honest with me. Why are you here?"

O'Connor leaned his elbows on the table and stared with sharp, shrewd eyes. He lowered his voice. "After I came back from the war, I bought a bar. Galway Saloon in the Mission District. Officially, it's a soda fountain. The bar's in the back."

"A speakeasy?"

"Some call it that. There's a fellow who runs a couple of ships up and down the coast. Whisky from Vancouver. He sends my shipment by rowboat to a cove north of the bay. Every month I pick it up here and drive it back to the city."

"Aren't you afraid of getting caught?"

"This isn't like New York or Chicago. There's no consolidation, no mobsters. West Coast bootleggers are small beans. We pick up what we need for our own purposes. Usually, the feds leave us alone."

"But something went wrong this time."

"Rain. Too much damn rain. My car got stuck like a tar baby. Twenty-six cases of whisky in the hold." He shook his head. "And now the heat is on. Prohibition agents seized a guy's truck and shipment in Sonoma last week. They're looking for rumrunners. I can't afford to get caught."

"What are you going to do?"

"The only thing I can do. Leave the car. For now. I covered it up with branches as best I could. When the storm lifts, I'll get it unstuck and be on my way with no one the wiser."

"Except for the Widow Baker." She cocked an eyebrow and leaned forward. "Do you carry a gun?"

His eyes flashed in the light as he stared at her. He reached into the loose waistband of his pants and pulled out a Colt revolver in a leather holster. He placed it on the table with a metallic thud. "We all do. For hijackers."

She looked at the weapon on her table. "Have you shot a man?" she asked, shocked at the unseemly fascination in her voice.

"Lots of 'em." He picked up his glass and took a long drink of milk. "Only I was wearing a uniform and doing it for Uncle Sam." When he finished his meal, O'Connor cleared and washed his own dishes. He wiped his hands and turned to her. "I saw a Victrola in your parlor. Could I start it up? Some music might drown out the sound of this rain."

"I usually stay in the kitchen when it's cold. There's no heat in the other rooms."

"I could start a fire for you."

Helen shook her head. "The chimney's stopped up. There's a furnace in the basement, but it's broken."

"Broken, huh?"

To her surprise, O'Connor rolled up his sleeves and left the kitchen. A moment later, he hauled the heavy phonograph into the kitchen. The sinews of his forearms bulged. Helen stared for a moment before she dropped her gaze, angry at herself for her girlish, visceral reaction to his body.

He wound up the contraption and for the first time in nearly two years, music filled the house. "Let's dance."

O'Connor took her hand and pulled her away from her work.

She shook her head. "I can't dance."

"A pretty young thing like you? I refuse to believe that."

On a dance floor of black-and-white tile, O'Connor led her in a foxtrot, a two-step, and a waltz. Even in his stocking feet, he was a strong lead, comfortable in his skin, and when she didn't know the steps, he made her feel like she did.

"Your cheeks are red," he said softly.

She rubbed at her face self-consciously. "That always happens. It's so ugly."

"No, it ain't." He pulled back and looked at her. "And red hair, too. Irish?"

She nodded. "My mother made the crossing."

"I knew it." He smiled to himself. "I came over when I was ten."

Burning under the heat of his gaze, she let go of him and changed the record. An upbeat tune filled the kitchen. O'Connor taught her the Baltimore, a shuffle he said was all the rage in San Francisco. When she stumbled forward into his arms, he embraced her, laughing, and a thrill passed through her. The clothes O'Connor wore still held the ghost of her husband's scent, but underneath the rough cotton was a different man, hard and hot and alive.

The record stopped, and the needle brushed the label with an insistent, rhythmic tap. She froze and looked up into O'Connor's eyes. His smile faded.

"Missus," he murmured softly.

"My name is Helen."

"Suits you. Helen of Troy."

She snorted. "Hardly."

"Helen of Half Moon Bay."

She liked the silly sound of it, the way the letters took shape in her mouth as she whispered the phrase to herself. She was just to the B sound when O'Connor pressed his lips against hers, stunning her.

Her first instinct was to give him a hard shove. So she did.

He hit the backs of his thighs on the edge of the kitchen table.

"What's the big idea?" she snapped. She checked the buttons of her blouse and fussed with her hair. Her hands had begun to shake. She tasted the salt of him on her tongue. "I'm not that kind of woman."

"You don't have to be any kind of anything to enjoy kissing." O'Connor was smiling and breathing hard. He took a step toward her again.

She took a step back, flustered. "Th-They came here asking permission to court me, you know. Six months after Peter died. Young, old, ugly, handsome. I turned them all away."

"Why'd you do that?"

"I didn't want another husband."

"I'm not asking to be your husband." He took a second step toward her.

She froze. "Then what are you asking me, Mr. O'Connor?"

"A gorgeous woman like you? Don't be daft. What do you think I'm asking?" With a wolfish smile, he closed the gap between them and took her in his arms.

She could feel the tautness of his body as he crushed her against his chest. Not a single soul had touched her in two years. Her deadened nervous system lit up like a chandelier.

"I'm asking to take you to bed."

"The hell I'll let you." But her voice was weak.

"I'll make it good for you." The hot promise boiled her blood. "Helen."

Trembling with desire, she looked at him. "Oh, God."

"Say yes." He reached up and rested his heavy hands on her shoulders. He skimmed his thumbs up the sides of her neck and tipped her head back so that she could look him in the eye.

"Yes," she whispered.

"Jim." His voice was rough. "Say, 'Yes, Jim.'"

Helen swallowed. "Yes, Jim."

Nothing gentlemanly lived in his second kiss. His open lips sealed over hers, tasting and tonguing her to mad pleasure until her body, divested of its inhibitions, melted against his. He tasted of salt, cigarettes, and sweet, smoky whisky. Her body screamed for the flavor. Closing her eyes, she bent into him, her belly pressing against the rock-hard erection in his trousers. His rough stubble scraped her chin. She buried her hands in his hair and groaned as he continued to kiss her, hard and slowly, unearthing feelings she'd buried long ago.

Still locked in a kiss, they took three faltering steps to the kitchen table. Jim lifted her and set her down on its surface. He ravaged her neck with kisses and dug his fingers through her hair. Loose locks tumbled down her back and hairpins fell like raindrops to the tabletop.

"You smell good enough to eat," he murmured in her ear. "Like violets and cakes and all sorts of sweet things."

He reached under her skirt and slid his hand up to the bare skin underneath her garter belt. His fingers made a bold foray underneath the loose silk of her step-in.

When she felt the hot caress of his touch between her legs, she gasped and grabbed onto his shoulders, almost collapsing backwards onto the table.

"How long have you stood there wanting my hands on you?"

His roguish voice was liquid sex in her ear.

"Dripping for me?" One more kiss and he slid to his knees, drew up her skirts around her thighs, and untied the wet scrap of silk between her legs. When he looked up at her, his eyes were lucent, like two shards of sea glass.

"What are you doing?" she whispered. Shame and lust mixed like a burning cocktail in her throat.

Instead of answering her, he grabbed her hips, pulled her to the edge of the table, and pressed a hot kiss on her trembling sex. Her fists tightened on his shoulders, and her body clenched hard. She tried to sidle away, but his hands were like vises on her thighs. He began to lick and suck on her aching flesh, building up a steady rhythm that alternately relaxed and exasperated her. His beard scraped her tender skin. Pleasure swirled in her body like electricity, mysterious and powerful. She could feel the warmth of his breath on her nakedness, the wet wickedness of his muscular tongue.

Once, in the middle of their honeymoon, Peter had taken her suddenly after her bath. Her body had seized around him in a furious series of spasms, both terrible and wonderful. Afterwards, as she lay on the bed panting, she asked, "What on earth was that?"

"That?" Her husband kissed her forehead. "Why, a paroxysm, dear heart. A little fit of feminine hysteria. Nothing to worry about."

Then Peter had gone off to war. And she'd never had a paroxysm again.

Jim worked her body, drawing lightning bolts of pleasure in the middle of a storm. Helen's mouth fell open, jaw slack, and her eyes shut tight. He found a tight knot of nerves and began to tongue it, again and again, until she was moaning like a ghost come back from the grave, desire surging through her veins.

Then it happened—the dam of pleasure broke over her, and she lost all control. She clawed at Jim's shoulders and shamelessly rode his lips as she convulsed, the most intimate part of her body pressed against his face as he looked up at her, his eyes bright with self-satisfaction.

When the waves subsided, Jim stood, and Helen noticed for the first time that they were both still completely dressed.

He cast a big shadow over her, and she gasped when he grabbed her and carried her up the stairs. When he kissed her, his mouth tasted like her own body, musky, salty, and sweet.

As they left the warm kitchen, the cold enveloped them, chilling the sweat on their faces. The electric light in her bedroom was dim, the radiator in the corner frozen and dead. The patter of raindrops grew louder.

"How do you stay warm in here?" Jim's breath was visible as he asked the question.

"I bundle up like a granny."

"Well, ain't no bundling up tonight, sweetheart."

He was a stranger in her house. But when he set her down on the bed, she reached for him and kissed him with all the passion her body could summon. She unbuttoned his shirt and ran her hands under the cloth, feeling his hot skin and hard muscles against her palms. He pulled the shirt off his shoulders, and she stared up at him, breathing hard. A light dusting of blond hair covered his chest, and his nipples, tiny as sugar pastilles, rode on pectorals as rigid as a strongman's. Feeling naughty, she reached up and lightly pinched a nipple. When he curled forward, all of the muscles in his lean torso flexed, gloriously, and Helen stared.

"Hey!" He laughed and pushed her backwards. The mattress springs brayed as she lay on her back, overcome by a fit of giggles.

Quickly, he stripped off his socks and belt and put a small metal box on the nightstand. His trousers were gone in the blink of an eye, and all of a sudden, Jim was standing in front of her, legs spread apart, his cock in his fist and a ravening hunger in his eyes.

Helen's smile fled and she licked her lips. She wasn't educated in such matters, but she knew enough to know that God had been generous with James O'Connor: long and thick and straight, his cock pointed at her like an accusation she was more than willing to accept.

"How long has it been since you've lain with a man?" he asked softly. An Irish accent had crept into his words.

"More than two years."

"We'll go slowly, then."

"Don't you dare."

Together, they unbuttoned her blouse and clawed at the clasp of her skirt until she was lying before him in nothing but her stockings and an untied step-in. He reached down and ripped the silk garment from her body, dropping it on the floor next to his pants.

When he slid over her, his bare skin seared her with the heat of pleasure. He swallowed her gasp with another kiss, and she lost herself in the languorous, unhurried strokes of his tongue. Her eyes slid closed, and she seemed to melt into the bedclothes, her body overheated and her insides twisted with sexual arousal. She stroked the hard planes of his back and froze when her fingers snagged over a patch of jagged skin behind his shoulder.

Slowly, he sat upright and turned around so she could see the old scar marring his perfect back. "Bayonet," he said softly. "I fought at Amiens." He didn't say anything else.

She lay still as he lowered his lips to hers again. After drinking deeply from her mouth, his kisses covered her neck and ran down the center of her chest. He grasped her naked breasts in his big hands, sliding the rough pads of his thumbs over her nipples and making her groan like an animal. His hot lips closed over her right nipple, and he suckled her tenderly, the soft sound of his mouth blending with the sound of his fingers stroking wetly between her thighs. She opened her legs wider, and he gently but firmly pushed a finger deep inside, drawing it in and out with a slow, insistent rhythm, stretching her and getting her ready.

Her whole body felt hot, a fire burning too high and too fast. She drew herself up on her elbows, and he released her nipple with a soft smack of his lips. Together they looked down at what he was doing to her. Jim stared, his lips parted as though he'd never seen anything so splendid in his entire life.

"What d'you call this part of you, Helen?" His deep voice vibrated in her bones.

She smiled. "My ma used to call it my 'Irish fortune.'"

They laughed, almost shyly, then grew quiet. Helen stared at his handsome face and hot honey seemed to flow in her veins. "What do you call it, Jim?"

He slid his hand away and gave his shaft a couple of quick strokes. His cock stood up straight and proud. He reached for the tin on her nightstand and sheathed himself quickly with what Helen recognized as a prophylactic.

"What do I call it?" he said with a smirk. "I call it heaven."

Without another word, he grabbed her hips and yanked her roughly across the bed. Kneeling down between her legs, he spread her thighs with his hands and, his blue eyes searing hers, eased the head of his big cock into her.

Helen grasped the coverlet in her fists and stared at him as he snapped his hips forward, burying himself so deep inside her that her brain couldn't separate the pain from the pleasure.

He leaned back on his legs and pulled her hips against him, pressing even deeper than Helen thought possible.

"Is this what you've been looking for, Helen of Half Moon Bay?" Now there was no hiding his immigrant's brogue.

He began to move his hips back and forth, drawing his cock in and out of her in slow, sensual thrusts that built up a madness inside that she'd never felt before. Smiling, he reached forward and stroked her face and her breasts. Her nipples hardened under his touch, and she squirmed against the inexorable rhythm and strength of his body. His chest grew slick with a thin sheen of sweat but still he didn't rush, content with giving her a slow, long, deep fucking that left her whole body throbbing with hunger.

And the whole time he spoke to her in his deep, quiet voice, "You opened that door and I got hard in my trousers. I thought I'd gone delirious with cold. I thought I was dreaming you. A red-haired angel with eyes like the Pacific Ocean in a storm. A face from heaven. And God forgive me, tits and a sweet, tight quim to tempt the devil. You don't even know how beautiful you are, do you? Ah, Helen. You daft little rabbit, you've no idea."

Suddenly, he climbed over her and kissed her mouth. He entangled his tongue with hers as he thrust harder and faster. The bedsprings screamed. He kissed her neck, and she grasped his solid buttocks. His cock hammered into her, jarring her senses and scrambling her brain.

He grunted for breath like a beast. "I'm not going to love you like a wife. Or a widow. Or a whore. I'm loving you the way you deserve it, Helen."

"And how's that?" she gasped, running her hands through his damp hair.

"Like a woman who needs it."

He pulled out of her immediately and yanked her to her feet. He stood behind her, put one hand on her hip, and with his other hand, pressed his cock into her from behind. Bending his knees, he began to thrust hard, bashing her ass with his rigid abs and drawing strangled sounds of pleasure from her throat.

Holding her hip firmly with his left hand, he reached forward and strummed her tender, aching flesh with his fingertips.

Helen spread her legs wider and grabbed the iron bedframe to steady herself. She could hear Jim's cock working in and out as her body grew even more slippery around him. The unchaste sound filled her ears. She was trembling, her nerves pulled tight.

A whisper in her ear pushed her over the edge. "*Cuisle mo chroí.*"

Pulse of my heart. Irish words. Old words.

At once, her body tightened around him, and she clung to the precipice, unable to breathe. Jim sensed the change and worked his fingers furiously between her legs.

"Yes," he whispered, kissing her neck. "Yes, *mo chroí.*"

She flew apart like he'd pulled the pin on a grenade. Her screams echoed in the empty rooms of her house as though Jim had performed an exorcism and set her ghost free. Pleasure, white-hot, poured through her veins from the flashpoint where their bodies were joined.

A half-second later, Jim gave her three brutal thrusts and froze. His cock jerked inside her, and he exploded with a broken cry, his grip biting into her hip and his breath hot and fast against her skin.

They came down together. He clung to her through the final drops of his release and kneaded her tender breasts in his hands. He kissed the back of her neck, again and again, and continued to whisper to her in a voice that could lull her deep into sin, "Helen, you sweet girl. You bright angel. How could you go so long without loving?"

Their lovemaking outlasted the rainstorm. When Jim's tin was empty, they lay down together, tangled in the bedclothes, panting and naked in the sweltering little bedroom. He kissed her softly and stroked her long hair.

She tucked herself under his arm and rested her cheek on his slick chest, breathing in the spicy, clean scent that rose off his skin. She yawned and closed her eyes. "You'll leave me in the morning." Not an incrimination, but a statement of fact.

He kissed the top of her head. "Before first light."

Sleep rose up to get her before the melancholy did. She dreamed of the silk dress she wore at her wedding, of dancing the waltz and the foxtrot and the Baltimore with a handsome stranger, of her mother's dressing table with its violet toilette water and cut-glass rosary.

When Helen awoke, sunlight streamed in through the windows. She sat up and felt the sweet soreness between her legs. She was still naked, but the bed was empty. As promised, Jim was gone.

She heard a soft hiss. Confused, she looked at the long-dead radiator next to the window. A series of soft clicks resonated from its metallic guts. For the first time since summer, the air in the bedroom was deliciously warm.

"I'll be damned," she whispered with a smile. "He fixed it."

Down in the basement, the furnace roared with vitality. Smiling to herself, Helen climbed the stairs to her kitchen to make coffee. The Victrola had been moved to its original spot in the sitting room. She peeked out of her front window. At the base of her driveway was nothing—no stuck car, no cases of whisky, and no Jim.

Helen brought her coffee into the sitting room. Still

wearing her silk dressing gown, she lifted the lid of the phonograph and began to wind it up when she saw a note pinned to the turntable.

Until next month, mo chroí. Enjoy the heat.

Helen threw open the curtains. Music played softly in her ears as she looked out at the endless ocean.

In a few weeks, Jim would be back for his next shipment—and she would be waiting.

The Highwayman Came Riding

Erzabet Bishop

MARISSA HUGGED THE well-worn book to her chest and walked along the dirt path toward the inn. The setting sun edged behind the bevy of trees in the distance, the only sounds to be heard were the chirping crickets and an occasional barking dog. The sharp tang of a wood fire tickled her nose, and she wondered if it was close to dinner time.

She'd been reading on a bench under a tree when she noticed the gradual absence of light. And the silence. The English countryside had its charms and it was easy to imagine striding through time, herself embedded in the landscape that inspired her favorite story. So far, the adventurous English romp her roomie had promised had yet to materialize. At least for Marissa. All of her sighing had been between the pages of her book.

She caressed the familiar cover, the worn leather binding as much a part of her as the black skirt and fitted tee with the logo of last year's Romantic Book Con. The aged tome went with her everywhere. But here more than anywhere else, she sensed a stirring that hadn't been there before.

The Highwayman. One of her all-time favorites and a serious object of her lust. His haunting presence had been a fixture in her dreams for as long as she could remember. The rest of her English major friends had obsessed about the illustrious Mr. Darcy or the brooding Mr. Rochester. Not her. Her desire was all about the danger. The thrill of what might be hiding just over the next horizon. Hell, that was probably what got her out here in the first place.

She fumbled with her ear buds and began to sing along to the tune from Loreena McKennitt's version, the words tumbling from her lips. It didn't matter if she got it right. She just wanted to experience the music and let the words caress her skin.

"The wind was a torrent of darkness among the gusty trees. The moon was a ghostly galleon tossed about on a cloud of seas. The road was ribbon of moonlight, over the purple moor and the highwayman came riding…riding…The highwayman came riding up to the old inn door." She hummed the accompanying melody and sighed. No one out here but her and her dog-eared book.

Just the way she liked it.

Alice was inside, no doubt allowing herself to be seduced by the innkeeper's handsome son while she made do with her own company. The vacation had seemed like a good plan. Initially.

"Come on, Mar. You love this crap. Of course, you'll have a good time." Alice batted her eyes and wrapped a strand of long blond hair around her finger. A coquettish smile curving her lips into a pout, she looped her arm into the crook of Marissa's, dragging her away from her position behind the register.

The bookstore was quiet. Early Sunday mornings were up until about one-thirty, then all hell broke loose. But she didn't want to think of that here. Not now. Not when the music rolled over her like a spell, drawing her back to the swashbuckling days when men were men and the thing between their thighs was either the pounding force of a horse or a good woman.

Damn, but she was ready to volunteer for that last bit.

Marissa trudged toward the inn, loath for her time alone to end. She loved Alice, but she didn't want to watch her fawning all over the innkeeper's son's muscle-bound arms and six-pack abs. The trees stood around her like silent sentinels dotted along the grassy landscape.

That she'd be spending her vacation alone was a shame. But then she glanced down at the book in her grasp. The volume had been her companion for more years than she could remember, and when she fell between its pages, she came alive. If only guys in reality measured up.

With a frown, she continued until she came upon something resting in the grass. A few footsteps more, and she peered at the object, considering its familiar shape.

"What's this?" Marissa bent down and as her fingers touched the fabric of the French cocked hat, a sensation of being out of place settled over her. She glanced about, her heart racing. Everything *looked* the same—only it *wasn't.*

The light shining from the inn had grown dim. Only small pockets of illumination flickered through the windows. The cars parked out front were gone, and she caught the whinny of horses from somewhere close by. The acrid scent of burning wood was stronger now than what she'd noticed earlier. A woman dressed in a bonnet and a long dress with an apron emerged from the back of the inn. She dumped something out from a large basin and hustled back inside, the sound of rowdy masculine laughter trailing out into the night.

Something was off. Her stomach lurched with a growing sense of panic. "What the hell is going on?"

"I beg your pardon?" A burst of hot breath and a horsey snort skittered along the back of her neck.

The voice wrapped around her like gossamer silk, startling her. Marissa gave a small yelp and spun around, finding herself face-to-face with the muzzle of a horse.

"Ugh."

She blinked. God, had she been so out of it she hadn't heard him coming up behind her? She squinted up at the rider and her mouth went dry. His profile, dark against the moonlight, made her nipples tighten and her lower body grow warm. He evoked every kind of fantasy she'd ever had involving horsemen right down to the skintight breeches covering his muscular thighs.

Thighs she shouldn't be looking at. That was it. She was dreaming. What other explanation could there be?

Who in his right mind would be running around the English countryside dressed like someone out of freaking *Outlander* minus the kilt?

Now, that *was* a shame. Then she could investigate what was underneath it. This was her fantasy after all. She gave her arm a pinch, wincing at the stab of pain.

Was it real?

Nahhhh. Not a chance.

"Who are you?"

"I might ask the same of you. Skulking about in the open with naught but scant covering."

Marissa held her book to her chest and tugged the earbuds out of her ears, letting them fall along her neck. "I'm here on vacation. My friend is inside having some fun with the innkeeper's son. I, on the other hand, was outside reading until it got dark. Now if you'll excuse me, I probably need to get back inside."

God, but he was hot. Marissa dug the toe of her flats into the grass. *Unless you want to undress me and fuck me senseless on the wet grass.*

The rider shifted in his saddle and dismounted. His boots hit the thick grass with an audible *whomp*. "I think you lie. Why would a lass be out here in the thick of night save to warn me?" His tone grew husky, and he brushed a hand against the side of her face.

"W-warn you..." she stuttered. Damn, she hated when she did that. But the look in his dark eyes was all hunger. The rugged cleft of his chin and the way his lips curved up at the edges spoke of humor and naughty intent. The scar near his left eye warned her of danger.

Oh my.

"Aye. To warn me of the Redcoats inside."

Marissa blinked. "Um. Redcoats?"

He pressed his lips against hers in a tender kiss, enveloping her in his arms. "I thank ye, lass. 'Tis a brave thing you did, sneaking outside in naught but your underthings to give me leave to go. I'll not forget it."

The burn of lust slid through her body, making thinking difficult. His hands snaked over her back, pressing her hard against his muscular frame. A soft moan escaped, and she found her lips captured once more. This was her dream. A highwayman fantasy made flesh.

"One kiss, my bonny sweetheart." He breathed against her lips, and his hands cupped her sensitive breasts through the material of her tee shirt.

She started to say she wasn't his sweetheart, then remembered she had to be dreaming and just let herself go. If he would just continue to touch her like that, she would be his sweetheart 'til the cows came home.

Her fingers curled into the folds of his cloak, and she swayed against the rogue. The heat of his body was welcome against the chill of the night air, and the hard muscles beneath his clothes made her want to surrender to his touch.

His lips moved along the side of her neck, all the while moving her backwards until the back of her knees touched what felt like a bench, and she froze. That hadn't been here earlier. Her bench was a considerable distance away. At least, she thought it was.

His erection pressed against her stomach, and he groaned into her hair. "Ah, lass. I want you."

She opened her mouth to speak but all that came out was a small moan of consent. Dreams were made for scandalous behavior, and she was all in favor of having it out with her hottie right here and now.

His knee slid between her bare thighs, the slight black skirt parting easily to allow him access. Her panties were damp with the slick juices of her desire.

"Will you allow me to taste your sweetness?" His fingers dipped low, brushing the top of her mound through the thin panties and skirt, causing her to shiver. "Such an undergarment…Such a womanly form. Not all bones and skin. You've got flesh a man can hold on to."

A flush crept up the back of her neck, and her stomach gave a funny little flip. He liked her curves? Most guys preferred the skinnier girls that were the norm and not her more ample form. Wait. Of course, he did. This was her dream, dammit.

"Yes…" Hooking her panties around her thumbs, she slid them down her legs and onto the damp ground. She turned in his arms and thrust her ass in the air.

"You know how to tempt a man, love." He ran his fingers along the smooth skin of her ass and slid a digit between her legs.

Marissa gasped as his finger passed over her swollen labia, stopping to press inside of her slippery opening. "Oh…"

"Yes…" He shifted behind her. "I would have you now, lass. If ya be willing."

She heard a rustle of cloth. "Please…" Marissa parted her thighs to allow him greater access, balancing on the arm of the bench. The only sound in the air was the nicker of a horse, the wind fluttering through the trees, and the sound of their breathing. It was intoxicating, and she'd never felt as free in her life. Anyone could walk out the back door of the inn and see them beneath the tree. It would be in shadow, but they were still out in the open. Exposed. The thought just made her wetter.

The soft head of his cock brushed against her opening. He thrust forward, sealing himself inside of her with one bold stroke. She was filled, her nipples tightening as he began to fuck her, the brush of his breeches against her naked ass even more of a turn on.

She stifled a gasp as his pace increased. His hands wandered along her form, pinching and caressing her breasts and her body until she was ready to come out of her own skin. Never had a lover made her feel so desirable, so wanted.

His hips moved, the length of his cock pulsing in and out of her center. His fingers explored lower until he found her erect clit and brushed against it. "Feel me, love. I'm nearly there."

Stars twinkled behind her eyes as her body shuddered around his length. Another brush of his talented fingers sent her flying. "Oh!" Marissa cried out, jerking her hips against him as she rode the storm raging inside. Heat flushed along her skin, and her body quaked with the wave of her release.

He held her against his chest as she trembled and

shook, his cock slowing as his hips jerked and the warm splash of his offering filled her insides with his seed. His arms wrapped around her as he came, hips bucking and whispering nothings into her ear. "Ah, lass…" He kissed her neck and slid from her body. The highwayman turned her in his arms and pressed his lips to hers.

A noise from the inn made them both look up, and he began to fix his clothing, in turn smoothing down her skirt.

"If someone should see you, lass. The Redcoats are merciless. Hide yourself until they depart." He kissed her and walked to the horse waiting patiently under a nearby tree.

The highwayman mounted the beast, and he sat gazing down at her, the moon bright and weighty in the sky. The road behind him stretched out wide and as she handed him his hat, he placed it on his head, stopping only to doff it toward her once.

"Keep good watch." He pressed a kiss to her hand and released it. The horse snorted, impatient to move.

"Will I see you again?" A flutter of hope centered in her belly, and with utmost certainty, she knew she would.

"Aye, lass. I should think so." He winked and the horse reared, taking him and his rider deep into the darkness of the trees beyond.

Marissa sat and picked up her book, watching as his form vanished from sight.

★ ★ ★

SHE AWOKE TO the awkward clearing of a throat.

Marissa blinked her eyes in the bright light of the sun and winced as the crick in her back sent a message loud and clear. "I must have fallen asleep."

"You did. I came out here for my morning jog and saw you. I, uh, wanted to make sure you were all right."

The man stood with the sun behind him, and she had to squint until her eyes adjusted to see him. "The sun..." She held up her hand to block it. God, she didn't know which was more mortifying. The fact that she'd fallen asleep outside, or that she'd had a sex dream out here in the open. Anything could have happened.

"Sorry." He moved and sat next to her on the bench. "You seem to have dropped these.

Her panties.

A random guy she'd never met was holding her panties.

Oh fuck.

God. She really did dream the whole thing. She fidgeted against the uncomfortable wooden bench and smoothed her skirt. Wait... But why the hell were her panties on the ground?

"Thanks." She snatched them from his hand, her gaze lowered. When her fingers touched his, a spark jolted her to attention. It was then she really looked in his direction. He was handsome, with a cleft chin and powerful features, so much so that he and the highwayman from her dream could have been one and the same, right down to the powerful thighs and the scar on the left side of his face. Now that *was* interesting.

"Do you always sleep on benches with your panties

tossed in the grass?"

Marissa thought of her highwayman. "I was waiting for someone."

"Now that's the kind of date a guy could dream about."

"A girl, too, apparently."

The stranger watched her, saying nothing, a keen expression on his face.

By God but he looked so familiar. "Have we met before?"

He nodded. "I think I might have seen you when I checked in yesterday. You're here with your friend, right? I'm Curtis. And you are?"

"I am. Marissa. Nice to meet you."

He chuckled. "Oh good. If you were going to say your name was Bess, I was going to have a heart palpitation." He pointed at the book. "Were you reading it?"

"I was." Her gaze met his and an awareness crackled. "It's my favorite."

"Funny. It's mine, too." He stood with a rakish wink and offered her his hand. "Would you like to go for a walk on the moors later? I hear they're splendid in the moonlight."

"I would. But on one condition."

"What?"

Marissa grinned. "You have to tell me how you got that scar."

Queen High

Cela Winter

THE BAYOU SALON on the *Mississippi Belle* was only half-filled at mid-evening, but some of the high rollers were beginning to drift in. Buckskin and flannel rubbed shoulders with broadcloth and linen against a backdrop of all the splendor King Cotton could buy.

Royce Prescott took a puff on his cheroot, stretching his long legs beneath the table. The cards flew under his fingers, a restless round of shuffle, cut, gather, shuffle, fan…just another overbred dandy idling away the time. A façade that fooled many.

Such as the young cub in the corner, shakily downing a bourbon-and-branch, looking sick. Minor sport, but a pleasant warm up for the action to come. The lad ought to be grateful to learn the lessons young, mused Royce. Never bet more than you can afford to lose—and make sure you know who you're playing with. Shuffle, shuffle…

He nodded to acquaintances in the crowd, some of whom looked put out—or alarmed—to see him. Shuffle, cut, shuffle. He pondered the prudence of a move from the river to another forum for his talents.

Behind him, a Yankee accent was blathering to a companion about the California goldfields, "By Jupiter, Cantwell, it's 1851, and a man must take—"

Royce looked up at the sudden halt in the verbal flow. Other conversations in the room died away as all took in the newcomer at the door. Without thought, he found himself on his feet, reflexively catching his chair before it toppled.

"Beg pardon, ma'am, this yere's the *gentlemen's* card room." A sunburned individual in frontier finery scraped a bow.

"And, I believe, the location of a nightly poker game." The lady's voice was soft, her gaze lowered, hands clasped before her.

A stout man spoke up, his high collar wilting with the heat. "That's right, Miss, er, Miz, er, ma'am. Might you be inquirin' for one of your menfolk?"

"I'm inquiring on my own behalf, sir. My intention is to play."

There were snorts, mutters, a guffaw or two in the crowd that circled her. Forget-me-not blue eyes grazed the assembly serenely, confident of being deferred to. Royce found himself glad he'd been among the first to rise at her entrance.

Dark gold hair sleeked back into a heavy chignon, gleaming like the satin of her violet half-mourning gown. The neckline was a trifle décolleté for a woman bereaved, he noted. Not that he minded the sight of pretty shoulders and a well-rounded bosom. As if aware of his thoughts, the intruder drew the black lace shawl more closely around her in an oddly alluring gesture.

"Well, now, Miz—"

"Delaney. Mrs. Richard Delaney. And I have no menfolk. I-I'm quite alone in the world." She paused, touching delicate fingers to the pearl and onyx crucifix she wore as a pendant, a portrait of gentle sorrow. "I do realize the irregularity of my presence and beg your forbearance, gentlemen. My late husband left me unprovided for. I must support myself as best I can."

Royce felt an unfamiliar pang of sympathy and an inner stirring to protect such courage and—. Wait. His eyes narrowed. There was something about her... He spoke up, "Well now, gentlemen, as the lady has called us, how can we do less than bow to the wishes of our guest?" This should prove interesting, he thought. Brief, but interesting.

A trio of would-be players departed with mutters of, "petticoat poker," and "don't know her place." An armless chair was furnished to accommodate her spreading skirts. Solicitous inquiries about refreshment produced a small glass of sherry. The fair one sat, smiling around as if welcoming them to her tea table.

"There is the matter, ma'am, of, er, your stake."

Five golden eagles were withdrawn from her velvet reticule and set in straight formation on the table.

"Very good. Prescott, you have the deal."

She played with a concentration almost palpable in its intensity. Right from the start, he sensed she'd sized him up as the player to beat. She was very good, he had to admit.

The shawl slipped from one shoulder. Little more of her bosom could be seen than previously, but the slide of the fabric roused thoughts of disrobing and the revelation of further expanses of creamy flesh. Something about the aura of unassailable virtue made him want to back her into a corner and thrust a hand up her skirts, just to see how ladylike she'd be then.

Mrs. Delaney looked up, catching his stare.

Deliberately, he narrowed his eyes, letting the thoughts show on his face. She appeared to take no notice, her attention all for her hand, but the lace slipped farther still.

She licked her lips and asked for another card.

His attention wavered as he thought of that pink Cupid's bow stretched wide around his cock. He shifted in his seat; the front of his trousers had grown very tight.

The evening wore on. Players folded, and others took their places. The heat in the salon was intense, and the air foggy with tobacco smoke. The men perspired openly. Mrs. Delaney produced a handkerchief and blotted her forehead.

Royce observed that her purse appeared flat and considerably lighter than at the start of the game. Time to move. "Gentlemen, and lady, let's call a recess," he announced. "Shall we return in half an hour?"

The crowd waited as the door to the card room was locked, and a guard posted before players drifted off in pairs and threes. Royce strolled away, his mind hard at work. His air, as always, was one of nonchalance. What a perplexing and extraordinary opponent. While many men claimed that all women were creatures of mystery, he generally found them to be easily read and thereby easily manipulated.

Not so with the charming Mrs. Delaney.

A dainty veneer over a core of steel, he reckoned. And unless he was greatly mistaken, which seldom happened, a woman of great passion. He wondered if she knew—society conspired to distance proper ladies from the pleasures of the flesh. He would make it his business, his very gratifying business, to introduce Mrs. Delaney to her own sensual nature.

He found her at the aft end of the Texas deck, staring into the waters below. An occasional light on the bank appeared to drift by as the *Belle* churned her way upriver.

"Mrs. Delaney, just the person I hoped to meet." She was smaller than he thought. He quelled an uncharacteristic surge of protective feeling.

"Mr. Prescott." The alto voice was cool, but she did not move away.

"Should you be here, by yourself, in the dark, ma'am? Riverboats abound with all sorts of riffraff and rascals."

"I'm able to take care of myself, sir. Perhaps it is you I should be warned against?"

They laughed together. She had no idea how close she was to the truth, he thought. The mental image of her naked beneath him, her face flushed, eyes hazy with wanting, made his throat go dry. He swallowed. "You are a conundrum, dear lady, and I am determined to solve the riddle."

She tilted her head in an inquiring manner.

"Here you are, widowed and, by your own admission, in such straightened circumstances that you must pursue a most irregular form of self-support. Why do you not marry again? You cannot lack for suitors."

"Why, Mr. Prescott, is this a proposal? It's so sudden."

The words were a pattern of what any well-bred woman might say, but he detected a hint of mockery. "I could only hope to be so fortunate, some day. I merely wonder why you do not do as most women would in your situation."

"But I am not 'most women.'" Her tone was arch but with a tiny edge. "I have little use for romance and none for marriage, an institution of convenience for men and of servitude for women. Widowhood has its advantages."

"Not all men are bad."

"No, but how does one tell before it is too late? And forgive me, sir, but from what I hear, you would not seem well qualified to assert the nobility of your sex." The laugh in her voice escaped. "Is that what you wished to speak with me about?"

"Ma'am, let me be forthright. I observe that, as capably as you have played this evening, you now lack resources for more than another round or two."

"I still have my jewels."

"But what if they are not enough? While you are

skilled, the cards are notoriously fickle."

"And your point is?"

"I would be willing to advance you an amount adequate to see you through some hours more of play."

"You do not strike me as a philanthropist, Mr. Prescott. You doubtless have some form of collateral in mind against the loan."

Her voice sounded strained, and Royce silently cursed the darkness that hid her features. "The surety I demand is…your lovely self, Mrs. Delaney." He waited, wondering would she flounce off, scream, or slap his face.

"For how long?" Her tone was crisp and businesslike. "One night?"

"For twenty-four hours," he countered. "To do with as I wish, to explore with full carnality. You will submit to me utterly."

"I see. Tell me, before entering into such a bargain, just how much am I worth?"

He named a sum, adding, "In gold."

"Ah, a small fortune." She thought for a long moment, before saying, "Very well, I accept."

"Let us be clear, then, dear lady. If you win, you get the pot—and your dignity intact. If I win, I will take both, with great satisfaction."

To reinforce his intent, he backed her to the wall, caging her against the siding with his bulk. He lifted her hand to press a lingering kiss on the palm and then leaned in.

She raised her face in expectation.

To keep her guessing, he dipped his head to inhale the scent of her hair, her throat, the pulse point behind her ear. With the tip of one finger, he traced the neckline of her gown, just a whisper of touch over her breasts.

Her breath caught in something like a sob and she ducked under his arm, putting a discrete distance between them. "What makes you so certain I will lose?" With that, she turned and glided away, leaving Royce to stare after her.

He'd been so confident of having the upper hand in the encounter; why did he have the sneaking suspicion he'd just been bested at his own bargain?

★ ★ ★

"Time to show your hand, Mrs. Delaney." Royce struggled to keep the triumph from his words. On the table between them, the last two players, was all the gold he'd given her as well as her set of mourning jewelry. He fanned out his cards: A straight flush, queen high.

Face composed, his opponent dipped her head in acknowledgement of defeat. "Well played, sir. I bow to your skill and luck." She rose from the table amid the buzz of the crowd. In spite of the mixed welcome she'd received, the atmosphere was conciliatory with many offers to shake hands and murmurs of, "damned shame."

"Wait, please." He plucked the pearl and onyx cross from the spoils and held it out, dangling from the chain. "Far be it from me to deprive you of the spiritual and sentimental comfort of an object that must be so dear."

She gave him an inscrutable look before stretching out her hand and allowing him to drop the necklace into her palm. Without another word, she swept out. Not until the last length of violet satin had disappeared did Royce realize that she still held her cards.

★ ★ ★

RESTLESS, GEMMA SMOOTHED down her dress, then her hair, for the twentieth time. Should she rouge? A glance at the mirror showed her cheeks were flushed, so why were her hands icy? By far, the larger part of her nervousness was sheer…eagerness. Too long had passed since she'd had a lover. Her lips felt fuller, her breasts tingled, warmth pulsed between her legs.

An interesting man, Royce Prescott. She'd been watching him since New Orleans, as had every female from the ages of twelve to eighty. Speculations were rife in the ladies' parlor. He was rumored to be of good family (which Prescotts did he come from—Natchez? Louisville?) but cast off for his wastrel ways. Mamas warned off their daughters, while the more worldly whispered of dark appetites and women ruined beyond redemption.

Yes, Mr. Prescott was very interesting indeed.

Striking rather than handsome with laugh creases around the cognac-colored eyes, every gesture indicated considerable sensuality. It showed in the way he savored a sip of whiskey and the caressing gestures as he handled the cards. The thought of those elegant, long-fingered hands making free with her body almost caused her to stumble in her pacing of the room.

The rebel life she'd chosen, going against society's norms, required strength, determination, and loneliness, a state that warred with her body's desires. She burned inside for a man, for a firm hand and commanding voice—but only as far as the bedroom door.

Since last night, she'd relived their encounter on deck a thousand times, the hunger inside her ravening. She'd had all she could do to put him away from her and exit with dignity, resuming play as if nothing happened. He probably thought shock over his advances was what caused her defeat. She knew the art of losing well—as a set up for a greater victory. The hardest part was not to laugh at the end of the game. He'd been so smug, certain he'd bested her.

She would pay the forfeit gladly, whatever it entailed. She would take her pleasure as he took his and be on her way.

It was time.

The corridor, all flocked wallpaper and lamplight, stretched before her. The *Mississippi Belle's* mighty steam engine thrummed, the vibration rising from the deck and through her body to form a counter tempo to the pounding of her heart. She kept her pace deliberate, resisting the absurd notion that she was advancing to meet with fate.

A gentleman approached, his lady on his arm. Would he recognize her from the card room? She shrank against the wall, gaze lowered. The couple passed by without a glance.

She stopped outside his door, willing her nerves to settle as she tapped on the wood.

The door was wrenched open. "Yes?" he barked, barely looking at her, peering over her head down the hall. "What is it, girl?" He was in his shirtsleeves. Without his frock coat, she could see his trim waist and muscular thighs.

"Really, Mr. Prescott?" She pushed past him into the room and shut the door behind her. "I thought you a man of greater observation." She laughed up into his confounded face. "An apron and a calico dress make a rather thin disguise."

"Very clever. A gentlewoman is notable, a servant girl is…"

"Invisible. I do have a reputation to uphold."

"I assure you of my complete discretion. Shall we begin, Mrs. Delaney? Rather, I will call you by your given name, but remain Mr. Prescott or sir to you."

She bowed her head. "Yes, sir. And the name is Gemma." Outwardly meek, inside she shivered with secret delight.

"Remember, our agreement is that I may have every bit of you I desire, in any way, which I fully intend to do." A half smile quirked the corner of his mouth. "Charming as you look in that costume, I fancy I will prefer you out of it."

He stood so close that she could feel the whisper of his breath on her face. He smelled of soap, Bay Rum, and musk. He swept off the modest cap she wore. The pins that confined her hair were pulled one by one, the heavy mass shifting and slipping. His fingers combed through her locks, shaking them free to tumble down her back.

"A woman's hair unbound is such…an intimate sight." He sat, stretching out long legs in shiny brown boots. "Now disrobe. Slowly."

Slow indeed without her maid, but the simplicity of the clothing helped. Buttons, hooks, laces, and then she was stepping out of the circle of skirts and petticoats. She ventured a glance at her audience of one. His expression was impassive, but the amber eyes glittered. The fashionable stovepipe trousers clearly showed his arousal, which he made no attempt to hide.

More hooks undone and the pressure of her corset was released, allowing her the relief of a deep breath. Her lungs expanded, and the glow of desire spread through her from throat to loins.

"Keep going."

With a shimmy, she pulled the chemise over her head.

"Enough. Come close."

In pantalettes, stockings, and shoes, she stepped forward to stand between his legs. Naked from the waist up was somehow more vulnerable in comparison to his fully clothed state than if she'd been completely bare. It brought home the reality of how she had agreed to submit to him, a man she wanted and barely knew.

"Turn around." He made a circling gesture. "Let me see what I have bought." Royce examined her impersonally as if she were a horse he might consider buying.

"Stop." His gaze on her body was nearly as potent as a touch. A finger reached out to trace the creases left by the confining stays. She hissed, her skin exquisitely sensitive, her nipples puckering hard at the sensation.

He stretched out a calf and gave a curt nod. "Boots." A moment's hesitation, then she turned her back on him and took a wide step over his knee, straddling, and began to pull. He raised the leg still farther until it pressed through the crotchless split of her drawers. After the first instant of shock, she couldn't help the swaying her hips made.

"Do that again. Make that move with your oh-so-charming bottom."

Closing her eyes, Gemma rocked, her wetness slicking the column of leather she held snug against her pussy.

"Tempting as it is to take you here and now, we'll both enjoy it more for being postponed. Pray continue." His voice was thick when he spoke.

Task completed, he pulled her to his knee, jouncing her as one would a child. One arm clamped around her waist, his free hand cradled one bobbing breast, eyes riveted by its movement. He ducked in, seizing the taut nipple in his mouth, suckling with strong, deep pulls.

Gemma wove her fingers through his hair and arched her back. Vaguely, she wondered if she was wetting the leg of his trousers. She was moaning softly, losing herself to the pleasure by the time he pushed her to the floor, regarding her with challenge. She stared back, wide-eyed.

"Must I remind you that you are fully in my control, Gemma? Our bargain overrides any sensibilities you may harbor."

"It's not that, sir." She gave a saucy grin. "I was merely drawing out the anticipation."

There was an edge to his voice as he said, "You'll pay for that impertinence, but I'll let you wonder how and when. Carry on."

She started with his shirt, unable to resist the need to see his body. A scattering of dark hairs on his chest invited her touch. She tugged on them slightly, then more smartly, before grazing her nails down his skin to his waistband, watching the brown nipples pebble to hardness. His eyes glittered as she undid the buttons of his fly and licked her lips. He raised himself from the seat as she slid his trousers from his legs.

His cock stood straight up, pulsing in time to his heartbeat. Her pussy quivered in longing. One hand on the shaft, the other cupping his balls, Gemma rolled her tongue around his tip, absorbing the salty drop. Another lap and another, around and up and down his length, exploring each ridge and ripple, and then she stretched her mouth wide to draw him in. She felt him gather back her hair.

"Look at me." Obedient, she rolled her eyes upward. His face was flushed. "Yes, like that, but suck harder. Let me see that pretty throat working." She hummed with contentment, and she smiled to herself at his groan, knowing that for those few moments she was *his* master.

He cupped her chin and shifted to withdraw from

her mouth. "Very nice. I do love to see a woman enjoy what she has no choice but to do. However, now we must deal with another matter." His face was stern. "I ordered you to do something, and you were impudent. You took liberties. Such transgressions require correction. Go to the bed, bend over, and hold the bedpost."

She did as bid...and waited. He was trying to drive her mad, she thought. He moved quietly around her. From the corner of her vision, she could see him turning this way and that, studying her. She had a sudden image of how she must look—naked back, breasts, and hair hanging free, the split of her drawers revealing her most intimate places.

"Eyes down. You are only adding to your chastisement, Gemma."

As if following her previous thoughts, a finger parted the halves of linen and stroked the lips of her pussy, brushing so lightly over the hairs that a shudder passed up her body. The finger slipped in, dabbling in her silky wet desire. The touch continued, drawing up the cleft of her bottom, circling the tight pucker. Was that what he wanted, she wondered? So soon? Her pussy spasmed with disappointment. The finger was withdrawn.

The ties of the pantelettes loosened, and the pieces dropped, forming white rings around her shoes. A hand came down on her backside, making a crack in the still room like wood breaking. Gemma yelped at the smart. She should have expec—Another smack made her jump. Then another.

"This is what happens to girls who think themselves

above orders and discipline."

Steady blows landed on her buttocks and upper thighs. Her body was warming up. The pain was firing through all her nerves, expanding her awareness, translating to sensitivity in every pore and breath. Her legs were nudged wider apart, the finger exploring her once again.

"So wet. Seems the punishment is…pleasing."

Before she could register the movement, his hand swung away and the open palm landed a slap full on her pussy. She gave a shriek, and then found herself hoping for another, which didn't come. She heard a whimper and realized it was her.

"Tell me what you want, Gemma."

"Please, sir. Please…I need you." Her voice came out a breathless squeak.

"*Say* it. Say the words."

"Please…f-fuck me. Fuck me hard." She clutched the post and braced her legs. Her pussy was stretched wide and wider as he entered, but so slick and ready that her body offered no resistance to his girth. "Aahhh," she moaned as he moved within her, coarse hairs on muscular thighs rubbing against her delicate flesh.

Then he was gone, leaving her empty and aching for more.

On the broad bed, he lounged against the headboard, all but naked, his open shirt spread around him, his hand idly stroking his glistening cock. He pointed at the footboard.

Gemma scrambled up, wondering what would come

next.

He tossed her a pillow. "Get comfortable, and spread your legs."

She complied, tucking the cushion behind her for support.

"Frig yourself."

Her eyes widened, not at all what she expected.

"*Mind me*, Gemma. I'd beat you some more, but I fear you want that. What *I* want is what matters. Pleasure yourself. Do what you wish a man would do."

She'd never been so exposed, his greedy gaze roaming her body as she explored herself. Two fingers churned inside while her other hand flicked and circled. Her hips began to sway and lift, meeting pressure with pressure, her back arched—

"Stop!"

Adrift in sensation, she heard the word, but it didn't register.

He was across the bed in a trice, batting her hands away.

Gemma emitted a high-pitched grunt through gritted teeth, wanting to scream with frustration.

He fisted her hair, yanking her head back to face him.

Tears sprang to her eyes at the sudden pain.

His free hand wrapped around her throat with a suggestion of pressure on her windpipe. "You can finish when I give you leave."

Her whole body twitched with the pounding of her heart, her pussy fluttering deep inside from being confronted with such power.

As swiftly as he had pounced, he released her, retaking his position at the head of the bed. "Come here, my pretty equestrienne." He patted his flat stomach, his cock bobbing heavily. "Mount up, and ride like the wanton you are."

On stockinged knees, she straddled his hips, positioning him with one hand, the other on his shoulder. Taking a deep breath, she plunged down, impaling herself on hot, hard flesh. It truly was like riding a runaway horse—the power pounding between her legs, the mad beating of her heart, faster and faster, his strength carrying her along. Large hands molded around her hips, supporting her, helping propel her up and down. A searching thumb probed her split; guided by her gasps, he rolled her clitoris like a bead in oil.

"Please...*please*." Tears leaked from her eyes with the effort of holding back her climax.

"*Now*, Gemma!"

She arched back, straining...the tension snapped. Burning waves surged out from her center, concentric rings of white-hot ecstasy. Her inner walls clenched around him, held wide by his thickness. From a distance, she heard her voice crying out.

Relentless, he plunged on and on. Royce came with a shout, clutching at her buttocks to bore into her as deeply as possible.

She could feel the pulsing of his cock, matching the huffs of his breath. The sharp intimacy caught at her heart and pushed her over the peak again.

Spent, they sprawled amid the tousled bedclothes. Gemma's head was pillowed on Royce's stomach, a few inches from the resting length of his cock. She smiled to herself—there were still hours to go before their bargain was done.

"You're very good."

The rumble of the words through his belly into her ear made her chuckle. She undulated along his body, pulling herself up so their faces were even.

"Thank you, sir." She smirked. "I would say the same of you."

"Mmm, in bed, most definitely yes, but I was actually referring to the game. It took me a while to figure out how you did it, arranged for those cards to be in my hand. You are, dear lady, very good indeed." He rolled her over to her back, propping himself on an elbow to look down at her. "Men get shot for cheating at cards. So can ladies, I suppose."

"Somehow, I don't think any shooting will be going on here. Wouldn't that be something? You calling me out for cheating in order to get me into your bed?"

He laughed in reply. "Well, the appetites of widows are well known. Tell me, was there really a Mr. Delaney?"

"Ye-es, but his name's not Delaney, and he's not actually dead."

"Not a widow then."

"A grass widow, if you will. He was…not a kind man. I felt parting was best."

"So you've lived by your wits ever since. Remarkable."

The open admiration on his face made Gemma want to weep and shout with triumph at the same time. Having the acknowledgement of a true peer was a satisfaction as intense as their coupling.

The flare of emotion made her painfully aware that at the end of their twenty-four hours she would be on her own once more. The time that had seemed ample moments before became all too brief. She pushed away the idea.

Royce cleared his throat. "Have you ever thought of taking on a…partner?"

Her heart sank. Men were all alike—if they saw a thing, they wanted to own it.

"I neither want nor need a protector, some man to lord over me." It was difficult to appear haughty while lying naked in his bed, her bottom still tingling from his hands, but she did her best. "I will not be a possession."

"And I have not suggested such a thing. I'm offering, asking for, a collaboration between equals. Can't you see the advantages? We could work the river together."

In truth, there were so many places a woman alone could not go. Her entrance into last night's game was a bluff that had paid off.

"And if, *when*, things get too hot, we can move on."

Warming to the idea, she let her imagination roam. "Where? Out west?"

"How about Europe? Paris, Vienna. You'll be the toast of the town."

"While we steal the linings from their pockets!" They laughed together, giddy with exhilaration.

"You'll have a confederate in the drawing rooms of society...and a master in the boudoir. Though even here, Gemma, I think you have the upper hand."

His eyes darkened; the heat from his hardening cock pressed against her. He levered himself up onto all fours.

Her legs fell wide open, ready and willing for him to take her again. Then he was pushing into her, still sticky wet from their last encounter. Her head moved up and down beneath his thrusts, hair tangling in the rumpled blankets.

"Mr. Prescott, I think this is the beginning of a, *oh*, profitable, and most, *ohhh*, pleasurable, association."

Rogue Hearts

Delilah Devlin

JUST AS ARRANGED, I arrived at the hotel lobby at 8:00 PM sharp. I made my way to the concierge's desk and picked up the envelope left for me. Inside was the card key. No note. I headed for the elevators, trying to still the fluttering of butterflies in my belly.

Once the doors closed, I glanced at my reflection in the mirrored walls. Other than two bright spots of color riding my cheeks, there was no sign of my inner case of nerves. The woman staring back was a stranger: frizzy blonde hair tamed into a sleek, shoulder-length bob, features masked with artfully applied makeup, green contacts altering my ordinary, hazel eyes. The dress was another bit of subterfuge. The waist nipped in any softness there, the skirt flared over padded hips. The navy silk leant me an air of mystery and style, in stark contrast to my usual work "uniform" of fuzzy pajama pants and superhero tees.

Tonight was about fantasies—mine—and the packaging was just my armor to make sure I could get through this evening without geeking out. A tall order for someone as painfully shy as I was. Someone who preferred the company of her cat and her online friends.

The chime sounded as the elevator stopped at the seventh floor. I took a deep breath, lifted my chin, and stepped out with confidence. An act, because now the butterflies were flapping frantically to escape.

At the door, I quickly swiped the card, hoping I'd arrived first. So that I'd have time to get comfortable in my surroundings or hide in the bathroom. But when I pressed down on the handle, I heard music playing softly inside the pricey suite. The lighting was muted. A man wearing a tailored suit stood in front of the large window, his back to me, his lean frame outlined against the city skyline.

Should I clear my throat? I reconsidered. He might take that as a sign of nervousness. And I had been the one to select this particular scenario. No need to alert him to the fact this role I was set to play lay completely outside my reality.

He saved me from making my first mistake, turning slowly, his dark gaze roaming over my body.

As he looked, I hoped my jaw wasn't sagging. His profile picture on the Fantasy Dates forum hadn't done him justice. Tall and athletic, he'd written, but the description didn't encompass the breadth of his shoulders or the narrowness of his hips. His dark hair was cropped close, his dark brows a tad heavy, but they gave him that brooding look, that Heathcliff vibe that tended to cause a woman's knees to weaken and her heart to race. Mine sure did. Add lips that were neither too large or small, but with that requisite firmness that challenged a girl to think of a way to pull that mouth into a smile. He was utterly perfect.

Too perfect for me. I tightened against the urge to whirl and flee.

"You're prompt," he said.

"I consider it bad manners to arrive too early or too late," I murmured, wondering who the hell was speaking because my voice was never that sultry.

"Well, we're here," he said, waving a hand at the suite.

How was I to reply to that? *Duh. Yeah.* But then I realized what he wasn't asking. *What next?* This was my fantasy.

And what had I specified? *A good-looking male escort, willing to fulfill a new client's desires.* I'd been vague, and after my fantasy request had sat on the forum without a single query of interest, the administrator had asked if I could specify what those desires were. My mind had gone blank and for the two days I'd kept that website tab closed because I hadn't decided what exactly I wanted to have happen. But then, *he'd* replied. *Cool Operator* was okay with a vague scenario. He preferred room to "operate".

He'd saved me from having to put to words what I wanted. Now, I wasn't so sure that had been the wisest course of action. Our dark net forum was a place for the seediest, most secretive assignations. No Tinder or Match.com hook-ups there. I'd never had the nerve to put myself "out there" in a public way. Although I had questioned my sanity over going this route.

I took courage from my last reply to his arrangements for the evening. *My friends will know where I am. Should things go south, I'll be sure to leave plenty of DNA to point your way.*

He'd replied a moment later with, *Oh, we'll leave plenty of DNA, sweetheart.*

I'd spent a sleepless night contemplating that statement. Imagining the DNA we'd leave on the sheets, the rug, the bathroom...

Okay, so my fantasies had been strictly erotic. Not CSI-worthy.

And here we were, and he was still looking at me with those darkly hooded eyes, waiting for me to indicate how I wanted to proceed.

How would *Sonoma Siren* reply? *Keep to the script.* "Your agency said you were willing to accommodate special requests," I said, giving him a slight smile—hoping it was an appropriately seductive curve of my lips.

"My agency...was correct."

Still, he didn't move a muscle. Didn't approach. The moment dragged out until I knew he wasn't going to make this easy for me. His silence was a challenge.

Answering challenges wasn't something natural for me. Work came my way without much effort. I rarely ventured out of my routine. And yet, his brooding gaze sparked something inside me. Here, this night, I could be bold.

I strode toward him, letting my hips sway, aware the

fabric molded to first one side then the other, giving him a clearer idea of my true shape. His eyelids dipped as he followed my movements. His jaw tightened just a fraction.

My un-model-like physique didn't appear to put him off. My confidence grew. When I stood a foot away, I turned slowly. "Would you help me with the zip?"

He made a sound, like a soft cough, but his hands quickly lifted away my hair. The zipper lowered, and I took my first deep breath of the evening. He inhaled deeply and his fingers traced a path down the center of my naked back.

I looked over my shoulder, trying to gauge his reaction while at the same time flirting with my eyelashes.

He pushed the silk off my shoulders and bent to place a kiss in the curve of my neck. "I take it, we won't be heading to the dining room?"

"If you're hungry, we can order in…"

He bit my neck, causing me to jerk. "Maybe later."

I took an unsteady breath and stepped away. His hands left my shoulders. Turning slowly, I let him see the excitement building inside me. My cheeks were warm, my breaths jagged. I was going to do this. Have an assignation with a stranger. An "escort" I'd never met. And I was in charge. I lifted my chin toward his chest. "I'd like to see what I'm paying for." Well, we'd both paid for this, having agreed to split the hotel bill down the middle, but we still had parts to play.

His crooked smile was more bemused than salacious, a relief to me, because if he'd leered, I might have had second thoughts. Instead, adorably, a flush spread across his cheeks as he removed his jacket, his tie, then slowly unbuttoned his white dress shirt. The moment the sides opened to expose his chest, my breasts tightened. His chest was nicely muscled, lightly cloaked with dark brown hair. My gaze followed the narrow trail that disappeared beneath his belt.

He didn't make me wait. The belt, the zipper were both opened, the pants quickly slid down leanly muscled thighs. A runner, I thought as I tried not to gawk at the erection pressing against his gray briefs.

When he stood in just his underwear, his curled hands resting on his hips, I couldn't help but think of Bruce Wayne—urbane, handsome, cute in a suit—hiding his powerful allure. Not letting himself be seen for who he truly was until he masked up. Only *Cool Operator*'s attractions grew when he removed the safe suit. Did that make him Clark Kent? Imagining him nude but wearing a cape made me smile.

"Not fair," he said wagging a finger.

I took a ragged breath. "That should be my line," I said, waving a hand up and down his body. "I'm not nearly as interesting."

"I'm an escort. I've pleasured older women with neglectful husbands, homely girls who can't find their own dates. I'm feeling pretty lucky tonight."

A blush spread over my cheeks. But his reassurance did the trick. I stepped out of my heels, then pulled at the front of my dress, and slipped my arms out. Nude from the waist up, I gauged his reaction by the tightening of his abdomen and the stirring of the hard ridge poking at his underpants. Quickly, before I lost my nerve, I pushed the dress past my hips to let it fall with a soft whoosh to the floor.

I lowered my eyes and stood still. Suddenly shy. He stepped forward and reached out, his thumbs slipping under the elastic at my hips. He pulled. It gave. And then I was entirely naked, my thighs pressing together because a pulse was throbbing, there between my legs.

The script. I was the one in charge. I placed my hands on his hips, and glided downward, but his briefs snagged on his erection.

He made a soft grunting sound. I hoped it wasn't laughter. But the thought firmed my resolve. I plucked the waistband outward, freeing his cock, and then knelt to drag his undergarment to his feet.

Of course, that left his cock at eye-level—if I would only turn my head to look.

Slowly, his hand entered my view, and he wrapped his fingers around his shaft and slowly tilted it toward me.

Not the script. But what the hell? I was curious now whether it was as firm as it appeared. Whether I'd like his scent. Whether he'd taste every bit as yummy as he looked. I turned and tilted my head and let him press the tip against my mouth. I opened and invited him to slide the tip atop my tongue.

Again, his eyelids dipped. His features sharpened as his jaw tightened.

I slid my tongue over the crown and swirled and

swirled. Clean, maybe a hint of soap—his spicy musk was enticing. I latched my lips around him and sucked.

His head fell backward and he sighed.

Encouraged I was getting this right, I pushed away his fingers and wrapped my own around his length. I could be Sonoma Siren to his Clark Kent. A new superhero. A villainess ready to drain away his power—without the need for Kryptonite.

I sucked harder. My fingers tightened and began to stroke up and down his hard shaft, each glide rising to meet my downward moving lips.

His hips surged forward, pushing his cock deeper into my mouth. I gurgled a bit, but didn't resist, allowing him to slide along my tongue and butt against the back of my throat. Breathing through my nose, I relaxed and let him slide deeper, smiling around him when he groaned.

My own body warmed, melting from the inside. Moisture pooled between my legs. My nipples ached.

But just when I was certain I had him there at the precipice, he pushed me gently away and stepped backward. He reached downward for his slacks, pulled out his wallet and slid a condom from a hidden pocket. "Before we go any further," he said, his voice sounding strained.

I stood, watching as he rolled it down his length, ready to push him to his back and climb over his lap, but he scooted backward on the bed and patted the mattress beside him.

I wiped my hand across my mouth and lowered my

eyebrows. I didn't want to slow down. Didn't want to follow his direction. But I was also growing desperate to feel him inside me. Perhaps I could tempt him to give me what I needed if I were closer.

I crawled onto the mattress, firming my tummy, but allowing my breasts to sway. My best assets. Full, creamy-skinned, cherry-topped. And indeed, his gaze locked on my nipples as moved to his side and rested, propped on one elbow above him while he lay with his hands beneath his head.

"I'm curious," he said, his tone deep and a bit graveled.

I shook my head. "No personal details," I reminded him.

His gaze narrowed. Then he reached for a breast, plumped it in his hand, and rasped his finger across the tip. "Why this scenario?"

I drew a deep breath—partly because that lazy thumb was making me shiver, and partly because I wanted to share my answer. Still, saying it out loud... "I didn't want a date. Didn't want to sit across from anyone at a restaurant and make small talk, and at the end of the night, get a peck on the cheek and a promise to call. This is more direct."

He arched an eyebrow. "You wanted a hookup. I get that. But why use the forum?"

"I have certain desires I want fulfilled. And I wanted a player willing to do whatever I requested."

He grunted softly. "Do these desires have anything to do with that duffel bag you dropped?"

I nodded. "You agreed to be mine. To do whatever I want."

"Is there a list of things you want?"

"No. But once you open the bag, I'll expect you to use what's inside."

His head tilted, and his gaze narrowed again as he studied my face. For a long moment, he stared. Then he rolled to the side and left the bed, striding directly toward the bag. He set it on the banquet table against the wall and unzipped it, then glanced back at me with a look I couldn't read.

I closed my eyes, because I didn't want his laughter or judgment.

"Stay that way," he said softly. "Keep your eyes closed."

Something thudded, and I realized he must have emptied the bag. God, I hoped he understood how to use the things I'd brought. I began to regret not being at least a little more specific. *"Someone with BDSM experience required!"* would have made this moment less anxiety-filled.

His feet padded closer. The mattress dipped. "Open," he said, his mouth beside my ear.

I gave a little moan as I opened my mouth to accept the ball gag. Now, I wouldn't have to worry about making conversation with this man. I mouthed it as he closed the straps behind my head.

A finger lifted my chin. I peeked upward to find him staring down at the black ball trapped between my lips. "Very nice. Now, be a good girl and roll over. I want you on your knees."

Oh my, that voice! Firm but not harsh. Naturally dominant. Or at least as I'd imagined a Dom might sound. I rolled then hesitated. If I came to my knees, the view I'd present couldn't be more unflattering.

Something rapped the bed beside me. *The paddle.* I shot to my knees, my embarrassment forgotten, my body trembling with excitement. The leather bands I'd purchased were buckled around my thighs. A hand pushed between my shoulders until I lowered my chest to the bed. Then he took my wrists, one at a time, and fastened them against my outer thighs.

When he'd finished, I felt a moment's panic. I'd allowed a stranger to restrain me. He could do what he pleased. And if his particular fantasy was something darker than what I'd envisioned, I'd be helpless to stop him.

The bed behind me dipped. Hands stroked over my bottom and the backs of my thighs. "This is what you wanted?"

I lifted my head and gave a nod.

I felt his breath against my ass a moment before his tongue slid between my cheeks, following the divide from just above my pussy, moving slowly upward in wet laps until he reached my anus.

I held my breath and cringed a little bit, quivering, but then his tongue touched me there. I jerked, surprised at how sensitive I was.

"Easy," he whispered. "I almost regret not letting you give me that blow job. I thought we might talk first.

But you seemed...agitated. After seeing inside your little treasure bag, I get it. We'll play. Then we'll talk."

His words removed my fear. He wanted to play. Then talk. He could hardly talk to me if he planned to do me bodily harm.

His hands framed my hips, and I felt his cock nudge my sex. He rubbed himself against me, his cock and balls rolling against my pussy, drawing moisture down my channel. Then he moved back.

From the corner of my eye, I watched as he picked up the paddle. One side was padded and covered in red velvet. The other was bare wood. Which would he use?

Velvet stroked my skin—roaming over my buttocks, my lower back. I began to relax until it left my skin.

The first thud was soft, muted—and directed against the fleshiest part of one of my cheeks. I tensed before another thud landed on the opposite side. Yes! I rubbed my chest against the cotton duvet, exciting my nipples, and concentrated on the heat his smacks produced. I'd read about the pleasure that could be derived from a paddling—in online ezines, in erotic books. Now, I understood it. Warmth suffused my ass then washed in a wave upward to fill my chest and heat my face. Blood surged southward to engorge my pussy.

And still, he paddled me, not missing a single spot on my ass or thighs, until I couldn't help but try to move my hips in shallow rocking motions, because I was becoming aroused.

The paddle stilled. Fingers parted my folds. One pressed inside my vagina and swirled. "Not nearly wet enough," he said with a tsk.

He gave me no more warning than that. The next smack was sharp and loud as bare wood connected with my skin.

I made a bleating sound and drool seeped around the ball. He spanked me again and again, and I wriggled, trying to anticipate where the paddle would land to make sure it hit the well-padded part of my derriere, but he was quicker, sneakier, following no pattern.

In the end, I surrendered, counting the blows until…it happened. He smacked my pussy, and I felt a feathering convulsion tighten inside my walls—I was coming!

Another wet swat, and I turned my head to rock my forehead on the coverlet as I groaned loudly. At last, he tossed away the paddle. Lips surrounded my clit. Fingers plunged into my pussy. My orgasm was no longer gently feathering—it was exploding!

I jerked my hips and made crude grunting sounds— all things I was aware of doing but couldn't help. My body wasn't my own. It was his. When he drew hard on my clit, I felt it expand like a mini-penis, growing excruciatingly sensitive as he mouthed and tugged on it, until I sobbed around the ball gag. *Too much. Too much.*

At last, he released my clit. Withdrew his fingers. The straps loosened, first those restraining my hands and legs, and then the ball gag.

I spat it out and collapsed on my belly.

He stretched beside me, leaning on an elbow. "No hiding," he said, pulling my hair.

Shyness overwhelmed me—the old familiar feeling that managed to cripple my ability to relate to men. Ridiculous given everything I'd invited him to do. I took a deep breath and slowly turned.

His features were no longer brooding. His expression was...softer. "I have a confession to make."

I lay on my back, my breath a little too shallow. What horrible thing would he tell me?

He must have noted I was tensing, because he cupped my breast again, toggling the tip, until the intimate touch worked its magic and I relaxed.

"You have very pretty breasts," he said, a smile curving the corners of his mouth. "I could tell they'd be full, even when you were wearing that baggy Thundercats tee."

I blinked, not understanding. Yes, I had a Lion-O tee—the "Lord of the Thundercats" being my favorite character—but the shirt was so old I never wore it for my infrequent jaunts to the post office or the store.

My heart pounded slow and heavy as I stared. He waited for me to figure it out, and the moment I did, I jackknifed to sit and pulled a pillow to shield my body. "Michael from IT Guru? You've been stalking me?"

He had the good grace to blush. "I promise, I accessed your webcam just the once." He grimaced. "And I accessed your history when you left your desk to get a cup of coffee. That's how I found the forum."

I gaped—icy cold, at first, then searingly hot as fury rushed through me. "You—you—"

He held up his hand. "I prefer to think I was protecting you, Mina. Anyone could have answered your query."

"*You* answered." My words came out in a harsh whisper. He'd played along. Pretending he didn't know who I was. Didn't know every damn thing about me. Hell, he'd seen the porn site that had crashed my computer. "Fuck."

He took a deep breath. "IT guru is a side gig. My real job is working for a cyber-crimes unit. I investigate sites like the forum when bad things happen."

"And this is how you conduct an investigation?"

"Hell no." He sat up and raked a hand through his hair. "If the director ever got wind of the fact I'd visited a site like that on my free time, I'd be terminated. But I had to be there."

I snorted. "Because you were looking out for me?"

The deep breath he released lowered his shoulders. "Yes."

My eyes began to burn. I was fucking tearing up when this asshole stalker was telling me how he'd followed me to the site—to take care of me? Was I really that pathetic?

I guessed from the lengths I'd gone for a single night of adventure, that's exactly what he thought. "So, this was all out of concern for me?"

"To keep you out of a predator's hands…"

I looked away, doing my best to still the tremors running up and down my body. "Well, I guess you did your job. Do you want me to post my review on your work site or at IT guru?"

"Mina…stop."

A shudder racked me. This time, it had nothing to do with the fact I was humiliated. My body was just giving an involuntary response to the firmness of his tone. Well, damn. My perfect hookup was just going the extra mile to make sure a lonely woman didn't end up on the evening news.

"I'm not here, in this bed, just because I wanted to keep you safe." He moved slowly, reaching out to push my hair behind my shoulder then crawling closer to cup my shoulders. "I liked the woman I met when I fixed her computer. I thought she was pretty, funny. I liked the way she blushed when I asked how a nice girl like her had a web history like that." His jaw firmed. "I knew right then I wanted to meet you."

"You're just saying that because you don't want me to feel any more foolish than I already do." I groaned and lifted the pillow to hide my face. "And you saw my new toys."

"I did more than see them, sweetheart."

That sexy drawl set my belly fluttering again. Slowly, I lowered the pillow. "I guess we should both get dressed."

He shrugged. "Seems a waste. We have this suite for the night." He gave me a tentative smile. "How about I order dinner—on me. And we can make a proper date of this."

"You want a date?"

"I want more than *a* date. But if that's all you'll share with me tonight, I'll be satisfied." He reached for my hand. "Just don't go running from the room. I didn't mean to make you feel anything other than…desirable. Because you are. Even when you're wearing a Lion-O t-shirt and fuzzy zombie pants."

I swung the pillow.

He laughed and pretended to cower as I beat him with down-filled softness. A smile twitched then spread across my lips. I tossed the pillow to the floor and pushed him to his back. I straddled his hips and grabbed his wrists, "forcing" them upward. That he let me while he wore a sexy half-smile did a lot a to restore my dignity.

His cock jerked against my open thighs. I halted, frozen for just a second, but his heavy-lidded gaze was all the invitation I needed. He was still into this. Into me. His erection was as clear a barometer of his interest as a woman could ever need.

"You have me now," he murmured. "I'm completely at your mercy."

"I'm not any good at this," I said, needing to state the warning label on the package he was about to accept. "I don't get out much. Don't talk to real people very often. That's why I did this. Just thought you should know."

"Think awkward silences are going to scare me away?"

"No, but I've been…busy with life. And I have all these…things I've been thinking about…"

"Fantasizing about?" He traced my bottom lip with his forefinger. "Would you think me a total perv if I said that turns me on? A woman hoarding all those dreams of pleasure... I can't wait to find out what I'll be doing next. Or who I'll be."

I bent closer. "I have this one... I'm in a hotel room with windows facing another tower of the hotel. The curtains are open, and every light in the room is on."

He glanced toward the windows. "I'm listening... But don't you think you need to adjust those?"

My response wasn't something I could hide. Fluid leaked to wet the side of his thick shaft. I moved off him, left the bed, and padded to the curtains. I opened them, then stood in front of the glass, naked for the world to see—or at least anyone glancing out their window from the opposite tower.

I looked at my reflection in the glass and shook back my hair. Then I turned and sauntered back to the bed, grinning as he chuckled.

Again, I straddled him and bent close, my hair falling to envelop both our faces.

His smile disappeared, and he reached to cup the back of my neck and bring me closer. When our lips were an inch apart, he said, "I've been dying to kiss you, but the agency has strict rules against kissing."

I waggled my eyebrows, pleased he was still playing. "You can eat a girl out, but you can't kiss her?"

"Kissing's more intimate."

"Afraid the clients will fall for you? Is your kiss your superpower?"

"Baby, Lion-O's got nothing on me."

The kiss began with smiling lips, but quickly changed to something hotter...and sweeter. When I drew away, I was shaking with need.

I rose on my knees and waited as he gripped his shaft and set the tip against my entrance.

His gaze was hot. His smile crooked. "Guess we're way past the point where we should make proper introductions."

"You're Michael. I'm Mina," I said, sliding slowly down his cock. "Nice to meet you."

Lady of the House

T. G. Haynes

JADE HAD JUST clambered through the open window when she heard the noise. She froze and listened. Nothing, apart from the sound of her own heart thumping in her chest. *Keep calm*, she told herself, *you're being paranoid. Just relax.* She took a few deep breaths and waited for her pulse rate to decrease. It did so rapidly; after all, she was used to dealing with such situations. She was just about to lean out of the window and call to her partner in crime, Alex Spencer, when the sound came again. She listened intently. On both occasions, she'd found working out exactly what it was impossible. It was so faint that only someone accustomed to listening for the slightest sound would have picked up on it. Jade was exactly such a person.

Lithe, athletic, and agile as a cat, for the past two years Jade Jones had made a living—of sorts—by breaking into properties such as Hamilton Hall, the mansion that she had just entered illegally. Jade was not your typical housebreaker. For starters, she only broke into properties that belonged to the rich and famous. On the whole, these tended to be grand country houses situated in the middle of nowhere.

Although occasionally, just for the thrill of it, she would break into a property in one of the more exclusive residential districts of London such as Chelsea or Mayfair. Her tactic was to wait until the property in question was vacant—due to the owners being abroad—then she would strike. Upon entering the property of her choosing, Jade would double check the residence was empty, then proceed to live there for however long the house was unoccupied. Usually, this tended to be only a week or two, but occasionally, she was lucky enough to enjoy a slightly longer sojourn.

Another reason Jade had become one of the most successful cat burglars in the business was that she only stole what she needed to live on. The only indulgence she allowed herself was the odd bottle of wine from houses that had particularly well-stocked cellars. Given that what she took was considered so trivial by those whom she stole from, most of her victims didn't bother to report the crimes. Some didn't even notice. The very few who informed the police only did so half-heartedly and never pressed matters when investigations failed to turn up a suspect. Besides being highly skilled in the art of breaking and entering, Jade knew she'd had a good run of luck. As she stood stock still, listening intently in the drawing room of Lady Caroline Hamilton's residence, she wondered if her luck was about to run out.

Holding her breath, Jade listened for well over a minute, during which time she didn't hear a sound. She had just decided her ears must have been playing tricks on her when a voice faintly whispered, "Is everything all right?"

Jade grinned. Although she had only been dating Alex for a little over six months, his voice still brought a smile to her lips.

"It's fine," she whispered in reply.

A pair of hands, clad in black leather gloves, grasped hold of the window sill. The next instant Alex's angelic face appeared as he hauled himself into view. He smiled at Jade and, though he was quite capable of managing himself, asked, "Any chance of a hand?"

Jade considered the request. "What's it worth?"

"A kiss."

Deciding that a kiss was fair recompense, Jade granted him his request. As their lips met, she closed her eyes. It was strange, though she had a reasonable amount of experience when it came to kissing, she marveled at how excited she felt every time she kissed Alex. The sensation was as if a delicious little electric current pulsed through her whole body, making each tiny hair stand on end. She dearly hoped the feeling would never end; it was so thrilling, so spine tingling, so exhilarating. And that was just when they kissed; when he touched her... Reluctantly, Jade forced herself to pull away.

Alex looked disappointed.

"Rule number one," she reminded him. "First, we check the house."

Alex sighed. "You and your rules."

"It's always better to be safe than sorry," she said.

"You're right," he conceded, before holding out his right hand. Jade grasped it, bore his weight, and pulled. As he clambered into the room, Alex appeared to lose his balance. In order to prevent him from falling, Jade instinctively put her right arm around his waist. As he steadied himself, Alex ensnared her and stole another kiss. Against her better judgment, Jade melted into the kiss. Though she knew they should search the house before enjoying themselves, she found it almost impossible to tear herself away. Sensing this, he risked tracing his right hand down the curve of her back. When she didn't resist, he lowered his hand farther and began to stroke the contours of her buttocks. She was just on the verge of giving in to her desires when she thought she heard the noise once more. She tensed and pulled away from him.

"What?" he said.

"Didn't you hear that?"

He listened for a few seconds, and then shook his head. "I didn't hear a thing."

He tried to kiss her again, but she prevented him from doing so. Determined to reconnoiter the house, Jade asked, "Which do you want to take, upstairs or down?"

"I don't mind," he said.

"You take the upstairs then."

"Okay."

In almost perfect synchronicity, they each took out their mobile phones. "Have you got yours on silent?"

"Naturally," he replied.

"If either of us suspects anything is wrong, we text one another, get out of here instantly and meet back at that stile in the lane."

"All right." He went to kiss her. She pulled away. He feigned disappointment. "Just one, for luck?"

Knowing where it would lead, she declined. "Ready?" she said.

"As I'll ever be," he said.

With that they set off and began to search the house.

Stealthily, Jade padded her way around all of the downstairs rooms—the dining room, the ballroom, the library, the sitting room. To her immense relief, she found them all empty.

Having heard nothing from Alex, she decided to check the servants' quarters, hidden away in the bowels of the building. Though they were empty, Jade couldn't quite shake off the feeling of being watched. There were also one or two signs of life that made her feel uncomfortable. First, an empty bottle of red wine sat on the draining board. Second, a wine glass was in the sink. Strange, she thought. In most of the houses she and Alex broke into, the kitchens tended to be left immaculately clean and tidy. Picking up the glass in her left hand, Jade examined it by the light of her mobile phone. As far as she could tell, the lipstick around the rim looked like it had dried some time ago. Placing the glass back in the sink, Jade assumed Lady Caroline had simply fancied a few drinks on her last night in residence before setting off for her penthouse in the South of France. Trying her best to ignore the feeling of unease in the pit of her stomach, Jade made her way back up the stairs and into the main body of the house.

She had just reached the foot of the sweeping central staircase that led to the bedrooms when she received a text from Alex. "All clear upstairs, so why not come and join me? I'm waiting for you in one of the bedrooms off to the left where I have the most fabulous surprise. X"

Half-suspecting what the surprise was, Jade hurried up the stairway. Upon reaching the upstairs landing, she glanced to her left. Given that there were six doors to choose from, she sent Alex a quick text, asking him which door he was hiding behind. The reply came back almost instantaneously: "Guess…X."

Jade tried to suppress the smile tugging at the corners of her mouth, but it didn't quite work. With six doors to choose from, the situation was rather like a naughty boudoir version of Russian roulette. Deciding Alex wouldn't likely opt for the room closest to the top of the stairway, Jade crept along the corridor until she reached the last door on the left. Upon doing so, she pressed her right ear against the door and listened. Over the course of her career as a cat burglar, she had learnt to differentiate between extremely subtle grades of silence and the silence that was emanating from behind the door in question was almost *too* silent.

Slipping her mobile phone into her back pocket, she allowed the fingers of her right hand to slide around the door handle. Gently, she applied exactly the right amount of pressure and turned the handle. Much to her disappointment, the room was empty, apart from a small single bed in the far corner.

Jade was just about to retreat into the corridor when she heard a faint noise behind her. With lightning reactions, she spun around just in time to see the door of the room opposite ease shut. On tip-toe, she padded across the corridor and gently re-opened the door. Though the room was pitch black, she had the distinct feeling that she wasn't alone. It was just like Alex to hide and try to spook her. He did so love his little games. She smiled, determined he wasn't going to catch her out on this occasion.

After creeping across the room, Jade opened the curtains a fraction. A tiny shaft of moonlight allowed enough light to reveal a large four-poster bed to her right. At first glance, the surface looked as if someone was lying on the bed, tucked beneath the sheets. On tiptoe, Jade made her way over to the four poster and reached out towards the prone figure. The instant her hand came into contact with what she had taken to be a person, she realized that she had been duped. It wasn't Alex at all, but a couple of carefully positioned pillows. The next second something hard—like the barrel of a revolver—was pressed into the small of her back.

"What have we here?" said a deep, husky voice.

Realizing she had been caught red-handed, Jade raised her hands. Her mind raced. "Please, I was just…"

"Just what?" the voice cut across her attempted explanation.

"Nothing," she mumbled.

"So you have no excuse then?"

She shook her head, feebly.

"I suppose I should call the police," the voice continued.

"Please don't," Jade said.

"Give me one good reason why I shouldn't?"

Without a second thought, Jade made her way over to the curtains and opened them fully. Moonlight spilled into the room. As she turned, she saw that her inquisitor was making himself comfortable on the bed. Jade smiled at him. "Are you ready for this?"

"I was born ready," Alex replied.

In light of his somewhat cocky answer, Jade treated him to a sensuous striptease. To begin with, she teased off her black leather gloves. Then, after stepping out of her flats, she undid the button that fastened her tight black trousers. Intent on making Alex pay for the way he'd tried to trick her, Jade turned her back on him before lowering her trousers to reveal her favorite lacy black panties. Wiggling her buttocks provocatively, she backed towards the bed.

Alex reached out to touch her.

She slapped his hand away and scolded, "Not yet."

Reluctantly, he withdrew his hand.

Rewarding him for doing so, Jade took hold of the zip that fastened her top. She teased it down a few centimeters, then back up, then down, then back up again, until Alex let out a little moan of frustration.

"What's the matter?" she said. "I'm not turning you on already, am I?"

"Yes," came the husky reply.

"Hmmm, we'll have to see what we can do about that then, won't we?" Jade pretended to give the matter some serious thought for a few seconds.

"I've got it," she said, snapping her fingers. "Why don't you take your clothes off as well?"

"Why do I get the distinct impression I'm no longer in control of this game?" he said.

"Because you're not," Jade said. As the words left her mouth, she leant forwards and feathered Alex's lips with a kiss.

He tried to caress her, but she broke away. Barely able to control his desires, he lunged forward, but she deftly stepped out of his reach.

Realizing he had no choice other than to obey his mistress's command, Alex shed his clothing. In no time at all, he stripped down to his boxer shorts. Sitting back on the bed he was just about to remove them when Jade told him to wait. "Why?" he said.

"Because you know how much I enjoy doing this."

With that, she knelt down in front of him, hooked her thumbs into the waistband of the shorts and, very slowly, lowered them a fraction of an inch until the root of his cock strained to be released. The sight caused her to giggle. It looked so wonderfully naughty. Regaining a modicum of composure, Jade became aware Alex was holding his breath. She looked up at him, coyly.

He glanced down at her.

As their eyes met, she continued to lower the shorts, freeing his lovely cock. As she slipped the boxers down past his ankles, Jade lowered her head into Alex's lap, which allowed her to plant the faintest of kisses on the tip of his penis.

Alex bit his bottom lip.

After discarding his underwear, Jade kissed his cock again and again. Each time her lips came into contact, it twitched spectacularly.

"I seem to be at something of a disadvantage," he murmured, huskily.

Jade stopped kissing him and, in a semi-serious voice, said, "We'll have to do something about it then, won't we?"

Barely trusting himself to reply, Alex nodded, eagerly.

Given his compliance, Jade rewarded him by getting to her feet and recommencing her striptease. Taking hold of the zip on her top, she lowered it to her navel, exposing her cleavage in the process.

Alex gulped and closed his eyes.

"What's the matter?" she said, feigning chagrin. "Don't you like what you see?"

"Yes," he replied, "very much."

"In that case…" Deliberately letting the sentence trail off, Jade stood upright and lowered the zip. As her top flapped open, it exposed her glorious breasts.

The sight of them proved too much for him. Unable to stand being teased any longer, he rose from the bed and showered her chest with kisses.

She tried to push him away but her heart was no longer really in it, she was enjoying his attentions so much.

Taking Jade's left breast in his mouth, Alex licked around the nipple, deftly exciting it with the tip of his tongue. As he did so, he stroked his right hand down her taut stomach until his fingers came to rest against the waistband of her panties. He paused, momentarily, and then dared to go even farther. Easing his hand past the flimsy waistband, he brought the tip of his middle finger to rest against the nub of Jade's already moist clit.

Her only response was how her breathing grew slightly shallower.

Taking this as a further sign of approval, he started to massage her delicate folds of flesh.

Inexorably, Jade felt herself starting to melt as his expert fingers pleasured and pleased and teased her. It was uncanny. Each and every time they made love, the experience was as if he magically knew exactly the right thing to do. On this occasion, for instance, he waited until her juices flowed freely before parting her lips and gently slipping the tip of his index finger inside her. The feeling was utter bliss. She tried her best to lower her head to kiss him.

Being perfectly in tune with her, he sensed this and broke away from tending to her breasts to grant her wish.

No sooner had their lips met than Jade felt herself teetering on the brink of an orgasm. Part of her wanted to wait until she felt his cock inside her, but then, suspecting she had that pleasure to come, she gave into the moment.

The intensity of the orgasm took Jade by surprise. As

wave upon wave of pleasure coursed through her thighs, the top of her legs began to tremble. She felt as if each and every nerve ending was at the mercy of Alex's wonderfully playful fingers.

Deftly, as he sensed the climax wash over her, he altered his technique slightly, caressing her softly, enabling her to enjoy every little shock wave of pleasure to the fullest. Only when her orgasm was fully spent did he suggest that they might be more comfortable on the bed.

Readily, she agreed with the suggestion. No sooner had she laid down on the soft sheets, his mouth tended to her once more.

With a series of fleeting kisses, Alex teased his way down her torso, like he was determined not to let the level of pleasure she was experiencing drop one iota. Jade was eager to reciprocate, but it was difficult given how much she was enjoying herself. Trying her best to focus, she had just managed to half sit up when she felt his tongue come into contact with her pussy. It was no use. Once more, she gave in to him. As the tip of his tongue deftly flicked around her already stimulated folds of flesh, she sank back into the soft pillows behind her. In order to stop herself from coming a second time, she tried her best to focus on the precise movements of the tongue that was pleasuring her. Initially, as it went up and down, she was able to do so, but once it started to go around and around, she lost track, until all she was aware of was the delicious sensation building between her thighs.

Whilst Jade's second orgasm wasn't quite as explosive as her first, it was equally enjoyable. Thrilling little pulses of pleasure sparked through her pussy, her thighs, and her lower stomach. How long the blissful feeling went on, Jade wasn't entirely sure for she completely lost track of time.

After what felt like an age, finally Alex ceased licking her. Taking hold of his hands, Jade pulled him up the bed until he was lying next to her. Given his expert oral attentions, Jade planned to reciprocate by sucking his cock. Kissing her way down his chest and stomach, she had just reached his groin when she suddenly sensed that they were no longer alone in the room. Turning her head, Jade looked across in the direction of the door. Initially, she couldn't see anyone, for that part of the room was lying in deep shadow, but as her eyes gradually adjusted, she made out the form of a woman standing just to the right of the open doorway.

To confirm her presence, the woman raised a lighter to the cigarette dangling from her lips. She lit the cigarette and took a couple of drags. Jade thought something about her manner gave the impression she was enjoying the show.

As if to confirm this, in a softly spoken voice the woman said, "Don't mind me."

Until that moment Alex hadn't realized that anything was untoward. As realization hit him, he sat bolt upright on the bed.

Guessing who the woman was, Jade said, "I can explain."

"I doubt that very much," Lady Hamilton replied. "Don't worry though, I'm not really interested in explanations."

"So what are you interested in?" Jade asked.

Lady Hamilton took a final drag on the cigarette. "What you're going to do next."

As the words escaped Lady Hamilton's lips, Jade and Alex exchanged a complicit glance. Just to be sure she had understood correctly, addressing her host, Jade said, "You mean…"

Instead of replying, Lady Hamilton crossed over to the bedside cabinet and touched her cigarette lighter to the wicks of the two candles that sat side by side thereon. She then sat in the chair beside the bed. "I thought a bit of extra light wouldn't go amiss. After all, I wouldn't want to miss any of the show."

A faint smile spread across Jade's face as she realized that she was in the presence of a kindred spirit. Glancing back at Alex, she said, "You heard the lady."

With a wicked grin, Alex took hold of his girlfriend by the waist and lifted her onto his lap. As he did so, Jade could feel his stiff erection rub against the cheeks of her bottom. She could tell Alex wanted to enter her straight away, but she didn't allow him to, largely because she was determined to put on something of a show for her hostess. She sighed as he massaged her clit.

Still feeling incredibly turned on from her earlier orgasms, Jade had to take a couple of deep breaths in order to focus. Having done so, she eased back a fraction until she felt Alex's hard-on nuzzle harder against her bottom. Then, naughtily, she rubbed her bum cheeks against his cock.

Whilst teasing Alex thus, Jade glanced in Lady Hamilton's direction to make sure that her host was enjoying the show. Given that Lady Hamilton's left hand had sneaked beneath the waistband of her skirt, Jade took this as a clear sign of approval.

Returning her attention to Alex, Jade sensed his cock wouldn't withstand much more teasing, as she could feel tiny little patches of pre-cum coating the cheeks of her bum. Raising her thighs a fraction, with a further tiny readjustment, she felt the tip of Alex's cock come to rest against the entrance to her pussy. She waited until he stopped fingering her, then she lowered herself onto his prick. It felt such a snug, perfect fit that a shiver of excitement ran down Jade's spine. She enjoyed the feeling so much she raised herself again, very slowly, then, just as slowly, sank back onto his erection. She repeated the action over and over until she found herself teetering on the verge of climaxing once more.

Sensing this, Alex suddenly increased the tempo. More than happy for him to do so, Jade met his energetic upward thrusts with downward thrusts of her own. Their thighs blurred as they began to couple in earnest. Jade heard a faint low moan. Naturally, she assumed it had escaped Alex's lips but, on glancing to her right, she discovered Caroline Hamilton was who made the noise. Somewhat surprisingly, the lady of the house had raised her skirt around her waist, pulled her panties to one side and masturbated furiously.

Jade was so turned on by the sight, she bucked up and down even faster. This proved too much for Alex. Grasping hold of her hips, he came with a loud cry. As his cock exploded inside her, Jade climaxed a third time that night. Her latest orgasm was no less spectacular than the earlier ones she'd experienced. Her whole body felt like it was aglow. Her pussy was on fire, her legs tingled blissfully, and she even felt slightly light-headed. She was, however, still in control of her senses enough to be aware of a stifled gasp. Looking across at her host, Jade was happy to note Lady Hamilton had experienced a satisfying climax of her own.

Several minutes passed before everyone in the room regained a degree of self-control. With a faint cough Lady Hamilton pulled her knickers back into place and re-adjusted her skirt.

As she did so, Jade and Alex curled up together on the bed. Cheekily, Jade couldn't resist asking, "So, my lady, did you enjoy the show?"

"Very much so," Lady Hamilton said. "But…"

"But what?"

"Strictly speaking, I suppose I should call the authorities."

After considering the remark, Jade replied, "I don't suppose there's anything we could do to persuade you not to?"

Lady Hamilton's eyes sparkled naughtily. "I thought you'd never ask."

Barely able to suppress a smile, Jade extended her right hand towards Lady Hamilton and invited her host to join them on the bed.

Billionaire & the Jewel Thief

Elle James

JT FLOATED AROUND the grand ballroom of the Chance Tower in downtown Dallas, restless, bored, and ready to leave before the party had even started. As a member of Dallas's elite, she couldn't disappear until later in the evening without drawing attention to herself. People were still arriving, dressed in the best New York designers had to offer. The same designers who clothed celebrities on Hollywood's famous red carpets.

Granted many of the Dallas elite did not look like celebrated Hollywood actors and actresses, but they came damned close. Hair was beautifully coifed, and sparkling diamonds graced their throats and cufflinks. Most of the jewels were real; some were not. And not every member of this select class of people could spot a fake jewel, even under a jeweler's loupe. JT had a knack for spotting a phony from a yard away. She'd spent much of her adult life learning to detect real from imitation as part of the training her father provided for her role as a society debutante. Also the fact he owned mines on most continents of the world producing diamonds and precious stones helped. When he wasn't drilling her on the difference between a diamond and a cubic zirconia, he and her mother spent their time traveling without her to his various holdings around the world.

Which left her to entertain herself. Rather than sit around and sulk, or throw a tantrum like many of her peers, JT prided herself in her ability to find opportunities to both pique her interest and challenge her mind, like a good puzzle.

Even now, she flexed her skills as she worked her way through the room. Margaret Lansing, the wife of mega-billionaire Herman Lansing, owner of practically every automobile dealership in Texas, wore a beautiful cubic zirconia necklace with lab-created rubies. In an excited voice, she exclaimed her husband had gone all the way to Paris to buy it just for her.

If only she knew it was a knock-off, she might question what Mr. Lansing was doing in Paris that he felt he had to spend pocket change to appease his wife.

JT wore a simple diamond choker and matching drop earrings. She'd selected the diamonds herself from her father's collection and had the best jeweler in London assemble them to her design. Designing jewelry was only a hobby. As the daughter of a very rich Texan, she headed up his philanthropies and had started a few of her own.

A waiter stopped beside her, and she selected a fluted crystal glass of champagne from his tray. Tonight's event was the grand opening of Chance Tower, one of the most elegant new skyscrapers to grace the Dallas skyline. The structure was touted as the most modern with all the bells and whistles and a security system with no equal. Billionaire Chance Montgomery had not only funded the project, he'd been involved as one of the primary architects and security system designers. He'd had a full team working under him throughout all phases of production.

As if just thinking about the man conjured him, she spotted the man of the hour step through the ballroom door and pause. JT had just taken a sip of champagne when her gaze landed on him. She blamed the flutters in her belly on the bubbly. The man had no right to be so damned handsome. He wore the tuxedo like the garment was graced to be on his impressive frame. Every female gaze swung toward him, and JT could almost hear a collective sigh over the music of the classic band in the corner of the ballroom.

His gaze swept the occupants of the huge room like a king surveying his domain. Well, it *was* his building, and he *was* the owner. But king?

JT snorted. The man was full of himself and could stand to be brought down a peg or two. Perhaps she would accept that challenge some day, but not this night. She had other plans that didn't involve spending her entire evening making polite chitchat with people who bored her out of her mind. As soon as she could leave with grace, she would.

Turning from Chance, JT merged with the crowd, aiming for the dance floor. As with most events involving the Dallas privileged, the music leaned toward the big-band era with the muted trumpet and saxophone playing soft, flowing tunes that showcased the sway of long skirts and the many ballroom dance lessons the guests had invested in.

One of her father's friends stopped in front of her. "JT, you look lovely tonight. Would you humor an old man and dance with me?"

Glad for something that didn't require her to stop and talk to every person in the massive room, JT accepted the offer and floated out on the floor to the beautiful notes of *Moonlight Serenade*.

"How is your father, JT? I haven't seen him in a while."

"He and Mother are at their resort in Africa. They should be back for a couple days at the end of this month before they fly off to Chile."

"How are you faring all alone? Are you finding enough to do to keep you busy?"

No matter that she had long passed the need for a nanny and had been living in her own apartment for the past six years, she endured being treated like a child to be entertained and watched after by her father's friends. She didn't mind. She'd long since discovered that she was the only person who could make herself happy and if she didn't have confidence in her own abilities, no one else would. She smiled politely. "I find enough to keep me busy, thank you."

They completed the dance in companionable silence, and JT excused herself. No sooner had she left the company of her father's friend than she turned and ran into a solid wall of black tuxedo and gray cummerbund.

CHANCE HAD SPOTTED her soon after he'd entered the ballroom. After making his way through a throng of well-wishers, he finally found her exiting the dance floor. "Ms. Trace, so good of you to come to the grand opening of Chance Tower." He stared down into eyes a deep shade of violet.

"Oh, cut the crap, Chance. I know you and you know me, you don't have to put on the air of a high-class billionaire." Her eyes narrowed. "I know your story."

He lifted her hand and brushed his lips across her knuckles. "Ah, JT, I can count on you to bring me back to my humble roots."

"And don't you forget it." She tugged, but he retained control of her hand and swept her out onto the dance floor, executing a perfect Viennese Waltz to *Moon River*.

JT couldn't be mad or argue when the man could waltz her heart right out of her chest. She lost herself in his arms as he whirled her in slow, sensuous turns around the floor. When the music came to a halt, she tried to remember why she was annoyed at him, but she couldn't. All she knew was that she had to get away before she made the mistake of asking him to take her to bed and make love as beautifully as he waltzed.

"Excuse me. I seem to have need of a visit to the powder room, and then I think I might call it a night."

"Bored already?" He lifted her hand to brush it again

with a soft kiss. "You shatter my ego."

"It must be difficult for a man of your stature to have such a fragile ego." JT tugged her hand free. "Congratulations on your new building. It's magnificent. I hope it's everything you designed it to be."

His eyes narrowed for a flash and then he was smiling, graciously. "Why thank you, Ms. Trace."

She hurried away from him, before the lingering traces of the waltz made her forget who she was and what she was about to do.

AFTER JT LEFT, the party seemed flat and boring. JT had a way of bringing the room to life with her quick wit and her talent for seeing through the bullshit of the upper echelons of Dallas society. Chance was a newcomer to the elite. Having achieved billionaire status two years earlier, he and his money had been welcomed into the secret handshake club at the top of the Dallas food chain. He hadn't wanted the notoriety, but it helped to grease the skids when he wanted a building permit for Chance Towers and when he needed the financial backing to fund the building until he could get it opened and operational.

Now that his dream had become a reality, he could fade back into the obscurity of his Texas ranch and enjoy what he liked best—ranching, riding, and raising horses. And he could spend a little more time with his friends, something he hadn't done much of since he'd begun the multi-billion-dollar project.

Chance wandered around the ballroom once more,

hoping JT had decided to stay after all. Unfortunately, she appeared to have left for good. He knew the party would continue on without him with free finger foods and an open bar. What he wanted was to find a place where he didn't have to smile incessantly and where he could relax for a couple hours before he headed out of Dallas, back to his ranch.

Taking advantage of his full access to any part of the building, he entered the private elevator that would take him to the one-hundredth-floor penthouse he'd leased to James Spillyard, the billionaire oil tycoon who owned most of the oil wells in the state of Texas and many of those in Oklahoma and who was tapping into Wyoming and North Dakota's vast reserves. The man had given Chance carte blanche on the design and décor of the penthouse with one stipulation. He wanted a state-of-the-art security system installed that was more robust than Fort Knox or the Federal Gold Reserve.

Chance leaned forward for the retina scan and waved the keycard with the embedded microchip over the chip reader. The elevator doors closed, and the car slid silently up the length of the tower, building up speed until it slowed to stop at its only destination. The doors opened onto a white marble entryway, with fifteen-foot Roman columns.

Before he took another step forward, he once again matched his eye to the retina scanner against the wall and waved the microchipped key card over the reader, disabling the invisible laser light, an early warning device. If someone without approved access to the penthouse attempted to enter the foyer, they would disrupt the light flow and set off a security alarm that alerted the staff on duty in the basement of the building along with the Dallas police department and the FBI.

Spillyard requested Chance install his prized Star of Eternity, the ten-carat blue diamond that cost him a whopping three hundred million dollars, in a bulletproof display case in the middle of his living room. Chance thought the rare diamond would be better kept in a museum or vault, but Spillyard insisted on enjoying his purchase on a daily basis.

Thus the incredibly tight security system. He'd tested the system a number of times before having the diamond brought in by an armored car and an army of security guards and policemen. The entire block had been cordoned off in the middle of the night to facilitate bringing the diamond into the building.

Chance stood at the display case and switched on the internal light. He had to admit the diamond was beautiful, cut in the shape of heart. The multi-faceted gem refracted light in many different directions, sparkling like the brilliant star it was.

Spillyard had yet to move into his penthouse, but everything was in place for him to arrive the following week—down to the most expensive bedding, towels, and bath salts along with a full selection of toiletries any man or woman could possibly desire.

Chance wandered around the penthouse, checking the functionality of the drawers in the kitchen, the electronically operated shades over the floor-to-ceiling windows. When the shades retracted, they completely disappeared into the ceiling, leaving an uninterrupted view of the Dallas night sky.

The bedroom sported a king-size bed in subtle shades of gray and white with a splash of red for drama. It was tastefully decorated in modern, calming colors. He could imagine himself lying in bed with a beautiful woman, making love in the subtle lighting well into the early hours of the morning.

The woman that came to mind was the one whose perfume still lingered on his hands and jacket. Chance inhaled again to recapture the sensual scent. He'd enjoyed whirling her around the dance floor for the brief length of the song, but he'd enjoy even more the experience of having her in his arms for the night. JT was intelligent, with a body that could stop a train, and tantalizing violet eyes that seemed to see right through the playboy façade he'd erected around his heart.

He touched a wall sconce on the far wall of the bedroom and a hidden doorway swung open. This was the room he'd had the most fun designing. The room was Spillyard's naughty secret. Inside was an array of leather-covered devices, slings, straps, and every kind of sex toy one could imagine from a cat-o-nine tails to a miniature jail cell with handcuffs affixed to the wall.

The contents made Chance uncomfortable and hot at the same time. He ran a finger across what appeared to be a leather pommel horse. He'd had the owner of a BDSM dungeon come up with the list of items to order and the contact numbers for where to find them. Some items he'd even had custom made to fit the more upscale nature of the penthouse. Instead of faux leather, he had benches and seats covered in the finest, soft leather.

Until he'd had the request from Spillyard to build the room, he had never set foot inside anything related to a BDSM dungeon. Now he knew more about it and found the lifestyle interesting and oddly titillating.

As he stood in the secret room, the cell phone vibrated against his chest. He dug the phone out of his inside breast pocket and noted it was the security office located in the basement.

He punched the talk button. "What's wrong?"

"Sir, we have a breach in penthouse security."

"I'm in the penthouse checking things out."

"Sir, we understand. We monitored your entry a few minutes ago. Did you forget that the laser lights reset to On after ten minutes of inactivity, unless you actively disable them?"

"I know that and I did not disable them."

"Did you step through the laser lights and disrupt them?"

"I'm not anywhere near them."

"Oh, well then, perhaps they are malfunctioning. I'll send up a team now to check it out."

"I'm up here; I'll check and let you know." Chance ended the call and exited the naughty room, the door closing softly behind him, blending into the wall so completely, a person wouldn't even know it was there.

He strode through the bedroom, the sound of his footsteps swallowed by the plush wall-to-wall carpeting.

When he reached the door leading into the living room, he saw a shadow move through the columns into the far end of the spacious living area.

He tensed, his body on alert. He had nothing to use for a weapon. The best he could do was sneak up on the intruder and subdue him using the element of surprise. Slipping out of his dress shoes, Chance eased out of the bedroom and hugged the wall as he moved toward what was the most likely target of any thief managing to get past his security system.

The Star of Eternity.

His pulse pounding, Chance dropped down behind a sofa and moved closer to the display case, one agonizing inch at a time. At one point he had to leave the concealment of the couch and cross to a loveseat before he was concealed again. As he made the move, he glanced at the floor-to-ceiling windows. With the black of night behind them, the little bit of light inside the penthouse gave it a mirror quality and he could see the intruder, dressed completely in figure-hugging black from head to toe.

The burglar crouched low beside the bulletproof case and held up something to the locking mechanism.

Chance tested that lock so many times he knew it was solid. The thief wouldn't open it without a case of dynamite.

Holding something in his hand, the bandit waved it over the lock and then lifted the heavy glass box, as if the case hadn't been locked at all.

Anger replaced trepidation. Chance closed the distance between himself and the thief, grabbed his arm from behind, and pulled it up behind his back. "It's not nice to take things that don't belong to you."

The intruder didn't respond; instead he stomped on Chance's foot and used his free arm to jab a sharp elbow into his belly.

Chance grunted and loosened his hold.

The thief made a break for it, racing for the door to the penthouse.

Chance leaped over the back of the couch, tackled the man, slamming him chest-first onto the hard wooden floors.

The body beneath him bucked and twisted and nearly unseated him, but Chance held on and rode him out until the person calmed and lay still. "Who are you, and how in hell did you get into this apartment?"

The body beneath him grunted. "Any burglar who knows what he's doing would be able to get past that pathetic attempt at security."

The thief's voice was higher pitched than Chance had expected, along with having a very narrow waist and the gentle swell of a feminine pair of hips. "What the hell?" He rolled her over and straddled her hips, pinning her hands above her head. She wore a ski mask completely covering her face. Her body was encased in a skin-hugging, black jumpsuit with a long zipper that stretched from her neck all the way down to her crotch.

She rocked from side to side, struggling to free her hands. "Get off me."

"Not a chance."

Tensing, she raised her knee and pounded his back.

Chance scooted lower, trapping her thighs beneath him, pinning her legs to the floor. "The security team is on its way up with a Dallas police back up. There is no escape."

"You have to be joking. I got into this place, I can get out."

"Not unless I let go."

She glared from behind the mask. With the lights set low, he couldn't make out what color her eyes were, but her lips were a soft, rosy pink. Not at all what he would have expected for a thief. They were positively kissable.

Once again she bucked beneath him and almost unseated him. Leaning over to pin her hands to the floor above her head made him practically lay across her body. Every time she bucked, her breasts rubbed against his chest, and the jolt to his groin made him more aware of the delicate position she was in. Having just exited a room where bondage and sex awakened desire, the female beneath him was doing nothing to lessen the hardness of his member.

If he recalled correctly, he'd seen a pair of handcuffs in the secret room. All he had to do was get her from the floor into the room without her knocking him out and making a run for it…with the Star of Eternity.

Mentally, he counted to three, and then he rolled to his feet.

She jumped up as well, taking a step or two backward.

But he was ready. Grabbing her arm, he crouched like a football player and plowed into her gut, forcing her to bend over his shoulder before he straightened.

She kicked and hit his back with her fists, until he wrapped his arms tightly around her thighs and held on.

"Put me down," she hissed. "I'll leave. You won't ever see me again."

"Sorry, you broke in. How can I be certain you won't do it again?"

Her body stilled. "I promise."

"A promise from a thief?" He snorted. "You must think I'm an idiot."

"Well, now that you mention it." Again, she pounded his back and pulled at the back of his jacket. "Put me down."

He strode through the penthouse into the master bedroom. "Be still, damn it."

"I will as soon as you put me down."

"Right."

She went into a frenzy of action.

Holding her legs with one hand, Chance swatted her bottom hard with the other.

"Oh!" she squeaked. "You didn't just spank me, did you?"

"I did, and I'll do it again if you can't be still."

She drummed his back again.

Her blows caused minimal pain, the padding of his jacket and shirt cushioning her blows.

Again, he slapped her ass. "I said stop!"

She lay over his shoulder for a moment, unmoving. "That hurt."

"It will hurt a lot more if I have to pull you out of

that jumpsuit and spank your naked ass."

"You wouldn't," she said, her voice less confident.

Chance smiled grimly. "Try me." He tipped the wall sconce, revealing the secret room, and stepped inside. When the door closed, he turned and hit the code to lock the door.

"What the hell kind of room is this? You're not going to…you can't…it's illegal…" The woman twisted and kicked, hitting his back with new ferocity.

"What's illegal is breaking and entering."

She grunted. "I didn't break anything."

"But you entered without permission. Once the police get up here, they'll take you to jail."

"Let me go, I promise I'll be good."

He set her on her feet and stepped back. "I can't. This isn't my place. If it was mine, I'd consider releasing you, but I can't afford to let you leave now that I know you're after the diamond."

"I just came in to look at it. I didn't steal it."

"Because I stopped you."

"Still, I didn't take it." The thief stepped closer. "Please don't turn me over to the authorities." She stopped in front of him and traced a finger along the hard planes of his jaw. "I'll make it worth your while," she said, her voice soft and coaxing, like a cat begging to be rubbed.

His cock jerked beneath his zipper. Chance was glad he'd chosen the long tuxedo jacket because it did a better job of hiding his growing erection. The thief couldn't know the effect her words and the silhouette of her black-encased body was having on him.

"Come on, let me out of here. I promise to be a good girl and leave."

"No. I'm turning you over to the police."

She ran her finger up the front of his shirt to the bowtie at his neck. "You don't want to turn me in."

"Yes, I do."

"If you did, you wouldn't have brought me into this place." She glanced around the room, her eyes shadowed, her lips full and luscious and…familiar.

Chance wanted to pull her into his arms and feel her body against his, the ample curves defined by the sleek jumpsuit almost as tempting as naked skin. All he had to do was take the zipper in his fingers and tug all the way down to reveal what was hidden beneath.

As if reading his mind, she raised her hand to the tab and tugged a little. A six-inch gap opened in the front of the suit, revealing milky white, flawless skin.

"You can't seduce me. I'm a man with morals."

Her soft snort called him out on the lie. "If you had any morality at all, you wouldn't have carried me in here. This is a den of iniquity, a place designed for sin. Where a man can act out all of his most wicked fantasies, and if I'm not mistaken, the walls are soundproof."

Chance's lips twisted. "They are."

"I could scream, and no one would hear me."

"That is correct."

"I prove my point. You are a man without morals." She dragged the zipper downward, exposing the swells of her breasts. "A man who can break away from rules, can ignore the law and release a would-be thief if she didn't actually steal anything." The zipper dropped lower, revealing a black, lacy demi bra, the cups barely covering the lower half of her breasts and pushing them up high and tight. "Tell you what. I'll trade you a fantasy for my freedom."

Chance swallowed hard, clenching his fists to keep from touching her. Doing so would be wrong. So very bad to take this stranger in the mask when only an hour earlier he'd lusted after the lofty Julia Trace.

The thief's hand paused at her belly button.

Chance caught himself leaning forward to see what was below the zipper line. With the hood covering her hair completely, a glimpse of the thatch of curls over her mons would give him a clue about the color of the hair on her head.

He sucked in a breath and refused to act on his impulse to reach out and tug the zipper lower.

"Not interested in my proposal?" She turned away before he could act and walked across to a glass case much like the one in the living room. Only this one did not contain a priceless diamond, and it wasn't locked. It contained a startling collection of whips, each a different shape, size, and length.

The thief lifted the glass, selected a cat-o-nine-tails and lowered the lid. Tapping the leather straps against her gloved palm, she faced him. "What have you got to lose?"

"My business, my reputation, and my freedom if I'm caught aiding and abetting a thief."

"The room is locked; it's just me and you. Who will know?" She handed him the whip and strutted one foot in front of the other to the leather-covered bench and glanced back over her shoulder. Her hand moved in front of her.

He imagined she lowered the zipper all the way down. His heart stuttered and then raced ahead, his cock straining against his own zipper. The leather in his hand burned into his flesh. He had to swing it, to strike her flesh and make her cry out.

She pushed the jumpsuit off her shoulders and let it drop down her back, catching on her hips.

All he could see was the smooth white skin of her back, and he couldn't remember anything more desirable. As if of their own volition, his feet propelled him forward, one step at a time until he stood behind her.

"Tell me what you want." she said, her masked gaze capturing his. "It's your fantasy."

Knowing the request was wrong, but unable to stop himself, he whispered, "I want to whip your naked ass."

Her smile curled upward. "Done." She pushed the jumpsuit lower, exposing the perfect, rounded globes of her bottom. With her jumpsuit bunched around her knees, she leaned forward and rested her hands on the leather bench. "I shouldn't have broken into your penthouse. You have every right to punish me."

He tapped the whip in his palm once. The leather of the nine straps was soft and supple, hardly an instrument of torture. He lifted it and slapped it against his palm harder this time, and the straps stung his skin, making his blood heat and his groin tighten.

"Stop teasing. I deserve your anger." She leaned low, presenting her ass for his pleasure.

Chance groaned, lifted the cat-o-nine-tails and slapped it against her skin.

"Seriously?" She laughed. "Perhaps you *should* call the police. You don't have the balls to punish me the way I deserve."

"Silence!" he commanded. "I will determine when to call the police and how to deliver your punishment."

"Mmm. That's more like it." Smiling, she wiggled her ass and waited.

Still dressed in his tuxedo, he felt a surge of power slam through him. He slapped the whip against her ass again, this time with enough force to leave faint red marks.

"Again. Oh please, Mr. Montgomery, I wanted that diamond. I'd have taken it had you not caught me."

Again and again, he slapped her, the red marks glowing.

The thief moaned, reaching between her legs to dip her fingers into her channel. "Yes. My ass stings, and I'm very wet, it would be so easy to take me and do with me what you will. No one will know."

"Indeed, who will know if I touch you like this?" He stroked her back with the whip, sliding it around her sides to brush against her breasts. "Or like this." Drawing the whip back along her spine, he traced her backbone all the way to the crease between her butt cheeks and lower, to brush across her anus and pussy.

She quivered, raising her bottom higher. He could see her entrance glistening, inviting him to thrust into her, driving deep.

"You have to promise not to break into this place ever again," his voice and his control strained.

"You'll have to make it more difficult. I might not be able to resist the challenge." She arched her back, raising her ass another inch or so. "Take me now in trade for my freedom."

Chance unbuttoned his trousers. His cock leaped out, hard, straight. He dipped his hand into a bowl on a nearby table and removed a foil packet, stripped away the wrapper, and rolled it down over his engorged member. "I won't let you go next time."

She laughed and braced her hands on the bench, holding tightly. "Ah, sweet freedom is only a fuck away. Take me while my ass still burns."

He held her hips in his hand and positioned himself behind her, his cock poised to impale her.

"Hurry," she said. "Before the police get here, or I won't have time to escape."

He thrust into her until he was fully sheathed, her channel constricting around him, holding him inside. Then he pumped in and out, aware of the time and the fact he hadn't called the security team and given them a status. She was right. Only a few minutes remained before they burst through the door and caught her. And he'd be buried inside of her, caught with his pants down and fucking the thief.

At that moment, his career flashed before his eyes,

and he didn't give a damn. All he wanted was to make love to this stranger in the mask until he spent himself. Then he would gladly let her go to disappear, never to return.

He thrust one last time, catapulting over the edge, as his phone vibrated in his pocket. Still buried inside of her, he fished his phone from his pocket and answered, fighting to keep his voice even. "I'm sorry. I forgot to call you back."

"Is everything okay? We have a team at the elevator, but the locking mechanism has been disabled. We can't get up there."

"That's good." He moved inside the woman, his cock pulsing, a most delicious feeling of satisfaction washing over him. "I'll unlock it in a moment. Everything is okay. I found the problem with the laser lights, and it's been fixed." Chance patted her hot ass and pulled free. He helped her straighten and turned her around to tweak a breast between his thumb and forefinger. "I'll be down in a few minutes to see my guests off as they leave."

"Okay, if you're certain everything is okay. I have the police waiting on standby."

"Call them off. It was a false alarm." He ended the call and dropped his phone back into his pocket. "I guess this is your lucky day."

"Mmm. You're right." She wrapped her arms around his neck and pulled him down to kiss her lips.

He thrust his tongue past her teeth and caressed hers. She tasted of champagne and her perfume wrapped around him. Then because he was in a hurry, he helped her back into her jumpsuit and zipped it up the front.

Before she could move away, he reached out and yanked the hood from her head. Long rich brown hair cascaded around JT's shoulders.

Chance stared into violet eyes and smiled, warmth spreading deep in his chest. "I'll see you downstairs in a few minutes. Do you need help getting back into your dress?"

JT shook her head. "No. I can manage." She rubbed her hand over her ass. "You're getting better with the cat-o-nine, but you really have to tighten up your security. Anybody can walk right in." Then she winked. "See you at my apartment later?" Her gaze shifted to the cat-o-nine tails resting on the bench. "Bring the whip, and I'll show you the right way to use it."

An Eye for Love

Cynthia Young

Lady Olivia stomped along the length of the drawing room in Lady Salfordton's house. "Anne, I know Lord Comstock stole it."

"How can you be so sure?" her sister asked.

She threw her hands in the air. "Lord Comstock has always admired the eye miniature. He's an avid collector. It's not very large. Easy for him to make away with it. And furthermore, he was visiting the day it vanished. Grandmother gave me that miniature before she died. I must get it back."

Anne met Olivia's gaze with a bland expression, appearing unaffected by the loss. "Accusing a lord is not a trivial matter. Are you certain the thief was him?"

"Yes, there is no one else who'd shown an interest the way he has. You're defending him, and you were in his pocket almost the entire evening. Don't tell me you're in love with him."

Anne gestured with her hand dismissively. "I will tell you no such thing. Besides, other people including myself have admired it on occasion."

"True, but one of the servants came across the man and he said he appeared flustered." Olivia raised her index finger. "He was coming from the direction of the room where I keep my collection."

"Did you bring the matter to Father's attention?"

"Of course! I did it first thing, but he wouldn't countenance the notion that Lord Comstock would do such a thing. And Father has no interest in my blasted eyes as he calls them."

"Well, there is only one thing you can do."

"What's that?"

"Steal it back."

"How? Do you expect me to break into his home and search through his belongings?"

Anne rolled her eyes. "I don't expect *you* to break into his home. Hire someone to do it for you. You should go see Mr. Branson."

Olivia's back stiffened. "Mr. Branson? How will he—of all people—be able to help me?"

"Mr. Branson is quite capable as an investigator. He's helped a lot of people."

The man was insufferable. Much too handsome for his own good. His light brown hair curled very sexily around his head and made her want to run her hands through it. He always cast sinful smiles her way and his chocolate brown eyes lit with some undefined emotion whenever their gazes met. He was also arrogant. No, she would not be going to Mr. Branson for assistance.

★ ★ ★

OLIVIA LET OUT a long-suffering sigh as the home of Mr. Branson came into view. The home was modest, unlike the man.

Over the years, they'd been in the same social circles since he'd become friends with her father. He attempted to engage her in conversation by asking about her interests, but her heart would start to race and she would remove herself from his presence at the first opportunity. He stirred up feelings in her better left buried. The last time she'd allowed her emotions to overrun her reason, she'd been led to disappointment and—she shook her head to clear the direction of her thoughts—best to keep things in the past where they belonged.

She peered out the carriage window. The streets were still quiet, and she stepped out, relief filling her body. Scandal and ruin awaited her if she were caught entering his home unaccompanied. But she needed to recover the eye miniature by whatever means available. Her grandmother had been given the miniature by a man with whom she'd had an affair. She later passed the item to Olivia as a reminder to mind her passionate nature. Her grandmother never knew that the reminder had come too late.

Olivia raised her gloved hand and knocked on the carved wooden door.

The butler opened the door and peered at her. "How may I be of assistance?"

"I'm here to see Mr. Branson." She handed the gray-haired man her calling card.

The man's brows furrowed as he raised his gaze

from the card to stare at her. "It's rather early for visitors, my lady." He looked around her as if expecting someone else.

A chaperone most likely. She leaned forward. "Please, it is a matter of importance. I wouldn't be here otherwise." No, she would never have come to the man's house if not for the fact there was no one else she could ask for help.

The butler glanced around uneasily then opened the door wide, gesturing for her to enter. He led her to a drawing room.

Her feet sunk into a thick Aubusson carpet as soon as she stepped inside. The room was elegant and not overly masculine. Perhaps a female relative had assisted in the selection of furniture. The furniture appealed to her, and she could see herself reading a book on the red velvet armchair by the fireplace. Mr. Branson's tastes were similar to hers, which was a discomforting thought.

HENRY THEODORE BRANSON stared at the case file on his desk, adding the final notes before he had it filed away, when there was a knock on his door.

"There is a Lady Olivia here to see you, sir. I know you don't like to be interrupted in the morning, but she said it was a matter of urgency."

Henry dropped his quill, splattering ink across the page where he'd been writing notes. Lady Olivia? It wasn't possible. "Who did you say?"

"Lady Olivia. She's waiting in the drawing room. May I also add that she arrived without a chaperone?"

Henry stood. "Thank you, Owens. I'll be there shortly."

"Very well, sir." The butler bowed and left.

Why would Lady Olivia come—unchaperoned—outside of normal calling hours? The woman barely spoke to him.

He drew out a handkerchief and rubbed the cloth on his ink-stained hands in an attempt to remove the smudges. A futile task. He left the study and strode to the drawing room.

Lady Olivia faced away from him. She was bent over, examining a cloisonné jar which sat on a small table.

He froze. What would it be like to have her bent over him in such a fashion? Immediately, the blood began to pound through his veins. He shook his head. If he didn't regain control of his thoughts, his attraction would become quite obvious.

He coughed to clear the knot that had formed in his throat. "Lady Olivia, this is rather unexpected. To what do I owe this honor?"

She straightened and turned to face him, her eyes wide. "I didn't hear you come in." She gestured awkwardly around the room. "You have some very interesting items."

None of the items in the room interested him as much as the woman before him. Lady Olivia was dressed in a light blue walking dress and matching bonnet. A large white feather curled around the bonnet toward her face, bringing attention to her cornflower blue eyes.

"During my travels, I always made a point of collecting unusual items as a reminder of the location. That piece is from the Ming Dynasty."

"The detail on the dragons is amazing."

He stared, mesmerized, as she traced one of the dragons with an index finger.

"Perhaps on another occasion I can show some of the rare antiquities I have acquired. I'm certain that is not the purpose of your visit today."

A blush stole into her cheeks. "No, that is not why I'm here. I'm here because I need you to recover a stolen item."

He put his hands behind his back and rocked back on his heels. Lady Olivia had come on her own without a member of her family accompanying her, risking ruin if she were caught in his home. She was always very proper and never did anything that would cause scandal. Whatever was stolen must be of great value.

"It's an eye miniature, and it was taken by Lord Comstock."

"Lord Comstock?" Henry scoffed. "Lord Comstock is highly regarded. No one speaks ill of him. Are you certain the item wasn't misplaced? Did you witness him take it?"

Her face turned a deeper shade of red. "I don't have any proof, but he'd taken a keen interest in it and was later seen by some of the servants leaving the room where it was displayed."

"Even if he was coming from that direction, it does not mean he stole it. He is considered to be one of the most honest, upstanding individuals in London society. I don't think he would steal from you when he has a tendre for your sister."

Her eyes sparkled in anger. "I am fully aware of his esteemed reputation. He is still a thief."

"If I were you, I would exercise caution before accusing a man as powerful as he is of stealing."

"Mr. Branson, if you're not willing to investigate, I will find someone who will or do it myself if I must. I can see my visit has been for naught. I will not waste another moment of yours." She turned away, hands clenched at her sides, and strode toward the door.

He should let her go, but she was likely to create more trouble for herself if she pursued this fool's task on her own.

He caught her as she reached the door and pulled her toward him. The scent of jasmine teased his senses, stirring him as it always did when she was near. She stared at him, her disdain evident in her features.

"I'll take the case."

"You will?" she said, surprise lighting her eyes.

"Yes."

Her chest rose and fell rapidly. She stared at his lips for a moment, then raised her gaze to his and licked her lips.

As an investigator, he gathered a great deal about people through observation. Despite her avoidance of him and fleeing when the chance availed itself, she was attracted to him. He'd imagined many a time what she would taste like, but she always pushed him away. The opportunity had never presented itself either. Until now.

He reached up and traced her cheek. Her breathing quickened, and her ample breasts rose and fell with each breath. The exposed skin above the gown flushed to a deep pink. Taking a huge chance, he stroked his hand down along her neck then along the edge of the bodice, skimming the soft mounds of her breasts. When she mewled, he cupped her breast and stroked the peak with his thumb.

He met her gaze, half expecting her to push him away. But, instead, she drew closer, arching her breast into his palm.

With a low growl, he pulled her close and covered her mouth with his. He felt her hesitation, then her surrender to his kiss. As suspected, Lady Olivia was passionate, and he was thrilled to have that passion directed at him.

He ran his tongue along the seam of her lips until she opened her mouth. His tongue met hers, and she moaned. His blood raced, and he drew her closer, longing to feel her soft curves against his body. Her thighs brushed against his erection, and he groaned.

Henry was quickly losing control. If he didn't put some distance between them soon, he wouldn't be able to stop. He pulled away, but Olivia wrapped her hands around the back of his head, digging her fingers into his hair as she thrust her tongue into his mouth. With a simple move, she'd made his escape impossible.

He pushed the spencer off her shoulders, letting it drop to the floor, and then tugged on the bodice of her gown until her breasts were exposed. She trembled as he laved one of the rosy peaks with his tongue while he rubbed his thumb across the other.

"Branson," Olivia said. The sensations Branson's hands and mouth brought forth from her body were unlike anything she'd felt before. She never knew a man's touch could affect her so. That first time had ended so horribly.

She arched her back as he trailed kisses from one breast to the other and began to lave it as he had the first.

His arousal pressed against her stomach, and she rubbed against it, eliciting a groan from Branson.

Things were progressing too fast, and she knew she should end it, but a part of her wanted to know if she could derive pleasure from the sexual act.

She gasped as Branson ran his hand along her inner thigh. She was in such a haze of desire and need she hadn't noticed the hem of her gown being lifted.

His finger rubbed against her nub, and she trembled. He claimed her mouth in a kiss as he stroked her. She thrust her hips in tune with movement of his hand, and tension built in the lower part of her belly.

Another moan escaped her, deeper this time, and Branson increased his pace. Gripping his shoulders tightly as her legs no longer felt able to hold her weight, she wished the moment would not end. That her time in the arms of this man wouldn't have to end.

There was a knock at the door, and Branson pulled away.

Olivia's hands shook as she frantically tugged her

gown into place. Except for the swollen lips and flushed complexion, she was again the aloof woman.

Branson cleared his throat and took some steps away from Olivia to create a respectable distance. He faced the door. "Come in."

"Sir, Mr. Hopson is here to see you." The butler glanced at Olivia. "I took the liberty of taking him to your study to await you."

Olivia turned to him with widened eyes. "I can't be seen here alone with you."

"Do not concern yourself. Owens, have my carriage prepared and take precautions to make sure no one sees Lady Olivia leave the residence."

"Yes, sir," the butler said before leaving to fulfill his requests.

Branson approached Olivia and enveloped her hands with his own. "Owens will collect you once the carriage is ready." He leaned toward her, unable to resist another taste of her lips before meeting with Mr. Hopson.

Olivia frowned, pulled her hands out of his grasp, and took a step back. "Thank you. And thank you for taking on the case."

He drew his lips into a thin line. She was formal and aloof again. Back to the Olivia that kept him at a distance.

He moved toward the door, stopping in front of it and glanced back at her. "I must see to Mr. Hopson. I will begin my investigation and call upon you when I have gathered enough information." He exited the room and closed the door, not waiting for Olivia to respond.

Olivia stared at the closed door. She pressed a hand to her lips. He'd wanted to kiss her again, and she'd managed to pull away. But, oh, how she'd wanted to feel his lips against hers. As soon as his lips had brushed across hers the first time she'd felt a deep yearning awaken. If the butler hadn't interrupted, she'd willingly have given him everything.

Then he would learn that she wasn't a virgin and look down upon her—reject her. She clenched her fists. She couldn't lose control like that again, ever, especially with a rogue like him. Such things only led to disappointment and pain.

When he came to call on her, she would make sure to have her sister, Anne, present. She could not risk being alone with him again.

★ ★ ★

HENRY RUBBED A hand across his face. He still didn't know what had possessed him to allow Lady Olivia to come along. Her black bombazine gown rustled with every step she took beside him.

"Couldn't you have worn something a bit more…practical? Something that would not announce our arrival from a mile away? You should've changed as I requested."

"You said we only had a few hours to search the room. I did not intend to spend what little precious time we have locating something else to wear." She waved a hand in the air. "Besides, it was difficult enough to obtain my sister's widow's garbs without getting caught."

Branson had met her at the rear of Lady Salfordton's home. She'd told her father she would be spending the night with her sister since it would be difficult to escape her father's home without being noticed. Fortunately, Lord Comstock lived nearby. Branson led her along the mews and less busy streets until they reached the rear garden gate.

He opened the gate and stepped aside to let Olivia through. The hint of jasmine assailed him as she walked past him. He shook away the image of Olivia naked on his bed the scent brought to mind.

He quietly locked the gate and tugged her behind a hedge. Although the light from the crescent moon lent little light to the garden, lanterns lit the paths that meandered throughout the grounds. Listening for the sounds of guests who might be wandering the garden, he scanned the area for servants and guests. The information he'd gathered indicated the old earl would not be at his residence tonight, but the lit lanterns contradicted that. What if the earl had decided to remain in his residence and host guests instead?

After being satisfied no one was about, he grabbed Olivia's hand and led her toward the back of the manor. The feel of her hand in his sped his heart. He longed to wrap his arms around her and cover her lips with his.

She crashed into him when she stumbled on some unseen obstacle. He steadied her to keep her from falling, bringing her body up to his.

"Are you all right?" His lips nearly brushed hers as he said the words, causing his blood to pound and his body to become aroused.

"Yes, I am," she said. Her breath mingled with his in the dim light.

For a moment, so brief he thought he'd imagined it, she smoothed her hands over his chest before pushing against it.

"I'm all right," she repeated. She ran her gloved hands along her skirts.

"Perhaps you should wait here."

"We've already discussed this. Many eye miniatures look similar. You'll have a difficult time knowing whether you have found the one that belongs to me."

He couldn't argue with her on that point, which was one of the reasons he'd allowed her to join him. The other main reason was the opportunity to be alone with her again.

He studied the back of the house and noted the window to the library had been left open. When he'd finagled an invite to the earl's home the previous week, he'd taken every chance to note the layout of the manor. The earl had also given him a tour. After expressing feigned interest in art and eye miniatures, the earl had conveniently taken him to his collection room.

"We'll go in through the library window."

"What? You want me to climb in through the window?" Olivia whispered furiously.

"Did you expect to get in through the front door and ask the butler whether you can view Lord Comstock's collection for a stolen item?"

Olivia huffed and glared. "Let's get this done."

"Stay close to me."

They crouched by the open window. The room had a few lit candles scattered throughout. It was enough light to be assured no one was in the room.

"Reach for the windowsill, and I'll help you get inside."

Olivia did as he requested, going on her toes to grab a hold of the window.

He clasped his hands together to create a foothold. "Place your foot here and I'll lift you up."

She looked up at the window then his hands and raised an eyebrow, as if doubting his plan. But, she put her foot in his hands and he lifted, pushing her up. Olivia scrambled the rest of the way into the room then poked her head out to peer down at him.

"I'm coming in." He grabbed hold of the edge and lifted himself into the room.

Henry looked about the room. There was something not quite right about this venture. Everything had been easy—too easy. The lit garden. The open window. The candles in the library. He shrugged. Nothing for it but to continue and hope their luck didn't run out.

He approached the closed door, careful to not make any noise, and opened it a crack and listened. No sounds came from the corridor. He opened the door farther and glanced down both sides. All was quiet. He pointed toward the right. "The collection room is this way," he whispered.

Olivia nodded.

They made their way toward the room, Olivia remaining close behind him. Though her steps made no sound, her gown swished rather loudly in the silence. Henry winced. Too late to do anything about the gown now.

The double doors to the collection room were open. When he'd visited Lord Comstock and had been shown the room, it had been locked. Was this a setup? Henry glanced behind his shoulder, peering into the dimly lit corridor. Henry felt uneasy.

Olivia had entered the room. "There's no one in here. Come, Mr. Branson."

Henry followed her in and closed the door behind him. He walked to a tall oak chest with a set of shallow drawers. "This is where he keeps the—"

"Let me look." Olivia propped a candle on top of the tall chest and opened the top drawer. Frowning, she closed it and opened the next. After opening and examining all the drawers, Olivia placed her hands on her hips. "It's not in the chest."

She glanced around the room and moved to a curio cabinet. Henry proceeded to open other drawers and cabinet doors as well. There were no more eye miniatures to be found in the rest of the room.

"It's not here," Olivia said, unshed tears glistening in the candlelight.

Henry sighed in frustration. "I'm sorry we didn't find it, but we should leave. The hour is getting late, and the earl is likely to return at any moment."

Henry slowly opened the door and peered out. "It's clear. Let's go."

★ ★ ★

OLIVIA MOVED ONTO the terrace and squinted into the darkness. The missive from Mr. Branson stated that he'd be waiting for her outside her sister's house at midnight. Not seeing him from her vantage point, she took the steps down and walked along the path.

"Hello?" she whispered.

"Over here," he called out from her right.

She made out his figure in the near darkness and approached him. The scent of his sandalwood cologne surrounded her. "What is it, Mr. Branson? The missive said it was important."

"It is important, but first—" He grasped her hand and pulled her close. "Mr. Branson is too formal given all that has transpired between us. Call me Henry."

Olivia's heart rate sped at the memory of Henry's lips on hers and his touch in his drawing room not two weeks ago. She gazed up at him and licked her lips, wanting him to kiss her again.

He stared at her in the semi-darkness, his eyes glinting with desire. Yet, although he held her close, he didn't make any move to kiss her.

"Henry." His Christian name on her lips gave her a little thrill. She rose up on her toes bringing her lips close to his. "Henry," she repeated.

Henry gave a low growl and seized her lips in a kiss. He wrapped his arms around her and brought her body up against his. He ran his hand through her hair, dislodging the pins that her maid had meticulously placed. His erection pressed against her belly, and she felt an answering throb within her. She thrust her tongue into his mouth, savoring the feel of his tongue stroking hers.

Henry pulled at the front of her gown to uncover her breasts. When his lips covered one sensitive peak while he stroked the other with his thumb, Olivia gasped and clasped his shoulders for support.

He angled her so her back was against the tree and began to lift her skirts. Cool air touched her heated skin that quickly warmed under his touch. Olivia reached toward the front of his falls and caressed his cock through the fabric.

Henry hissed. "You don't realize what you do to me."

Olivia trailed kisses along his jaw and neck in response as she worked on the buttons to his breeches. Once the last button was freed, she wrapped her hand around his erection.

"Olivia." Henry panted. "We have to stop."

Impossible. She wanted to experience true passion and pleasure at least once in her life. "No, I don't want you to stop."

She dragged her hands across Henry's back, feeling the tension in his body.

Henry buried his face in the crook of her neck. "Are you certain? I can still stop."

"I'm certain."

He positioned himself at her entrance. "I'm sorry. This hurts the first time." He thrust his penis into her and froze at discovering the lack of a barrier.

Olivia held her breath and stared at Henry—waiting for the rejection to come. After all, what man would want a ruined woman when the one whom she'd given her virginity to hadn't wanted her?

Henry met her gaze then captured her lips in a kiss as he plunged into her. Olivia moaned and met each thrust. She cried out when she'd reached her climax. Henry thrust a few more times and spilled his seed within her.

Now, the rejection will come, Olivia thought.

But Henry continued to hold her close, smoothing the hair off her face and trailing a path from her forehead to her cheek with his lips before claiming her mouth in another searing kiss.

He lifted his head to gaze at her. "Olivia, darling, will you be my wife?"

Olivia's breath faltered. She turned her face away. "You would marry me even if I-I'm n-no longer..." Her throat tightened, allowing no further words to pass.

He framed her face with his hands. "Olivia,"—he tilted her face, forcing her to meet his intense blue gaze—"I love you. Your lack of virginity is of no consequence."

A sob ripped out of Olivia as the years of bottled shame spilled out. She buried her head against his chest, the warmth of his body and the scent of sandalwood providing comfort and security, even as her body continued to tremble with the release of emotions.

"I don't go around doing this, Henry."

"I know."

"I b-believed myself in love with Lord Minett at

nineteen. He'd lured me in with beautiful words. H-He'd made me believe he held the same deep regard. But he'd only wanted to find out what deflowering a woman would be like, and I'd been the naive, foolish girl he'd targeted for the purpose." Another sob shook her body.

Henry held her in his arms, whispering soothing words in her ear. Once Olivia had calmed, he helped her fix her gown and hair as best he could. Henry placed his hands on her shoulders. "I didn't ask you to meet me just to lift your skirts. I need to tell you that I found your miniature."

"You did? W-Where did you find it? Who—?"

Henry sighed and handed over the miniature. "Your sister."

The breath whooshed out of Olivia. Her sister had taken it? "No, Anne would never do such a thing. We must straighten this out at once."

Olivia marched toward the house, clasping the miniature so tightly it dug into her palm. She entered through the back of the home with Henry following. They found Anne sitting in a settee.

"I've been waiting for you."

"Is it true? Did you take the eye miniature?" Olivia asked.

Anne stood and took a few steps before pausing to face Olivia. "Yes, I did. And, Mr. Branson, I left the miniature behind for you to find earlier today when you had come by to provide Olivia with an update."

Henry raked his hand through his hair. "Do you realize the great risk I took to your sister's reputation when she accompanied me to go through Lord Comstock's collection?"

"There was no risk. Lord Comstock was fully aware of what was happening."

"But, why?" Olivia's body shook at the betrayal.

Anne returned her gaze to Olivia. "My dearest sister, I have seen how you and Mr. Branson look at each other when you think no one is watching. For years. So I came up with the plan to bring the two of you together. Judging from your disheveled appearance, I'd say my plan was successful."

Her sister cast a smile in Branson's direction. "Can I assume that you will be speaking to Father in the morning to work out the marriage settlement?"

"Of course—if Olivia agrees," Brandon replied. He took Olivia's hand and waited for her to respond.

Olivia swallowed, blinking rapidly to keep tears from spilling onto her cheeks. She supposed she could forgive her sister for stealing the eye miniature in order to bring love into her life. "Yes, I will marry you, Henry."

Anne clapped her hands. "Excellent. In that case, I will leave you alone—but for only a few moments."

Henry grabbed Olivia as soon as the door was shut and kissed her. "I love you, Olivia."

Olivia met his gaze, seeing the love in his eyes. "I love you, too."

Roguishly Handsome, and Other Superhero Problems

Tray Ellis

"YOU AREN'T EVEN applying?" Velda paused to dunk one end of an almond-vanilla biscotti into her café mocha before nibbling it. "But you'd be an amazing doctor. You wanted to be a pediatrician. Or was it a podiatrist?"

"I wanted to be a pulmonologist, and no, I didn't apply. I've thought about it," Ariel said with certainty. "But it won't work. I have to be able to leave at a moment's notice. That's not possible if you're a doctor." She leaned forward. "But I can still be in the medical field. As a researcher. There's so much we don't know about how the body works. I can help people, but it'll be in a different way." She reached out for her cup of tea. Her hand shook a little and the tea sloshed out. "I already sent off my application packets to several grad schools."

"You did? Good!" Velda sat straighter in the booth. The sunlight slanted in through the window, and she squinted slightly at Ariel through her prim wire-rimmed glasses. "I'm so glad to hear it. I worried you might do something stupid and not go at all." She paused. "You applied to Bristlecone University?"

"Of course I did." Ariel wiped up the spill with a napkin. "It's my first choice. If I get in, then we can room together. Like we do now."

"My fingers are crossed!" Velda held up both hands, with double fingers twined together. "We can't get separated. We've been best friends since forever."

"And we're both one of a kind," Ariel added in a low, secretive voice. She and Velda were the children of families that thrived in the small, secluded farming town of Dovecote. Ariel had grown up feeling ordinary, along with all the other children, even though something unexplainable about the *terror* inclined special gifts upon a majority of the population. She'd anticipated going away to college with equal parts dread and excitement. Back home, being gifted wasn't unusual, and for decades all understood that bad things happened when the outside world took notice of Dovecote's peculiar population. Ariel glanced left and right, but no one was paying attention to them, and she settled back. "While you get a degree in education, I'll get one in science."

"You'd make a great teacher, too, you know," Velda said, a hint of reproach to her words. "If you wanted to do it. You don't have to shut yourself up in a research lab. Science seems so lonely. All those test tubes and centrifuges and late nights spent alone."

"Can't." Ariel sighed and looked out the window. People were walking by with purpose, each on their way somewhere. So many lives, and sometimes, they seemed so terribly fragile. She looked back at Velda. "I wouldn't last a month as a teacher. Who would watch the kids when I had to leave?"

"You could do it in Dovecote."

"Others back home can help even better than me. Out here, they don't have hardly anyone. Hasn't it seemed wrong to just always hide?"

"You know that's a complicated question." Velda sipped her coffee. "Would it be so bad if you let the police handle things? They're good at what they do. You don't owe anyone anything."

"Sometimes I'm the only one who can help." Ariel looked down at her tea. The mug was comfortingly warm in her hands.

"You couldn't have saved Charlie or Henry, even if you'd been there."

"Maybe. But if I'd been there, I could have at least tried. I always wonder what if." Ariel shivered and focused on the sunshine streaming in through the window. The day was too beautiful to dwell on sad remembrances.

"You always try to take on too much." Velda shook her head. "You should be able to follow your dreams, too."

"I don't go looking for trouble. It's just helping out with rescues. Maybe someday it'll be enough and I won't need to anymore. But if I don't, it just feels selfish." Ariel tried to sip her tea, but her throat constricted tightly. She held it in front of her face and breathed in the scented waft of steam.

Velda dunked her biscotti again, and they sat there in silence for a minute.

Ariel tried to imagine would it be like if she'd developed Velda's abilities instead of her own. Both were powerful and useful, but Velda's were quiet. Ariel's were not.

Velda leaned forward to speak again when they overheard the man in the booth behind them. He'd been speaking on the phone to someone, and now he related his information. "That was Jack on the phone. He's on the bridge, and he said there's some kind of punk-ass desperado in an armored truck crashing into cars. The police are throwing up roadblocks, and Jack is caught in all the traffic. He said we shouldn't wait. I think we should get out of here before all the roads are clogged."

"I agree," said a woman, and a moment later, they both stood up and headed toward the exit.

Velda sighed. "You're going?"

Ariel dug out her wallet and extracted money to pay for her drink and then a little extra. She pushed it toward Velda. "Yeah. I can't ignore it, can I? Would you mind picking up some bananas on your way home? I ate the last one for breakfast this morning."

"Just come home safe," Velda said. She stared at the money but didn't touch it. "You aren't invincible, you know." She brushed a loose strand of hair behind an ear with one hand. "And it's your turn to take out the recycling for tomorrow. Don't forget. I don't want to hear any excuses about being tired."

Grabbing her backpack, Ariel rolled her eyes. "I've got my book club tonight. You don't think I'd miss that? I'll be home before dinner." She turned and dashed away, looking for a suitable place to change clothes. The bathroom of the café—one room with a small upper window—seemed perfect.

Very little time was needed to strip off her clothes and change into her costume. The backside of the door also had a full-length mirror and Ariel paused to check herself over. Unlike the heroes in the comic books, she dressed with practicality in mind. She almost always wore her black construction boots with steel toes, for the rare case where she might need to kick something. In her backpack, she kept a pair of black cargo pants, a black T-shirt, and a thick black windbreaker. It got breezy when she took to the air. She also wore a three-quarter helmet with a clear, partial face shield. Masks, she had discovered, were troublesome and did not protect one's head.

She pulled her dark brown hair up into a ponytail, plunked on the helmet, shoved her regular clothes into the backpack, and opened the window. A moment later, she was airborne. First, she scooted straight up and dropped off her backpack in a corner of the roof. She would return later and collect it. Then, she scanned the horizon, determined where the desperado was causing trouble, and headed straight out.

As the ground zipped by below her, people gawked at the sight of a flying girl. Several minutes later, Ariel slowed and hovered. There was a bozo in an armored truck. He was past the bridge now, but he'd left behind him a swath of dented vehicles. A police blockade was springing up downstream from him, but he'd smash through unless they had more time to finish setting up.

Ariel put her hands on her hips and considered the situation. She had no desire to get in the way of the police. Her intentions had always been to provide assistance with rescuing people. Although her natural talent was telekinesis, she wasn't trained to respond to active scenarios. Fighting a bad guy directly would be more than beyond her skill set.

Except, she was horrified to watch as the armored truck smashed into another vehicle. Bits of glass streaked everywhere. The clash of metal on metal vibrated down her spine, and the scent of exhaust fumes and dripping vehicle fluids seared her throat. She had to do something!

Again, Ariel glanced to the police blockade. She might not be able to stop him directly, but she could probably delay him long enough to let the police finish the job. Flying was one thing, and a skill she'd been practicing so long that it seemed second nature, but other manipulations required extreme focus. She extended her awareness and focused on the truck. Against her will, it careened into another vehicle, once again sending glass fragments flying and ripping metal and plastic to shreds. There were limits to the amount of weight she could heft with her ability, and an armored truck was far heavier than she could control.

She looked to the police blockage again. Perhaps she didn't need to do anything other than distract the driver using bluff and bluster. With a knot of anxiety in her stomach, she flew after the bad guy.

Determinedly, Ariel swooped down and landed on the hood of the car. "Hey, buster," she yelled. "Stop that truck, or I'll do it for you." Through the windshield, she could see the utter surprise on the ne'er-do-well's face. His strikingly handsome face, with chiseled features and penetrating eyes. He looked like he should have been modeling for a high-end magazine, instead of causing havoc on the roads.

The surprise was quickly replaced by drawn-down eyebrows and a devilish look. He mouthed some words.

Although Ariel couldn't hear them, it was pretty easy to read his lips: *make me*.

Then, the armored truck sped up, and Ariel glanced behind her. He was headed straight for the backside of a pickup truck. Ariel narrowed her eyes and shook her head. Okay, so he was calling her bluff.

She launched back into the air and twisted around. Now she was behind the armored truck. She couldn't move the behemoth by itself, but maybe she didn't need to. There were controls in the cabin meant to make operating it very easy.

First, she wobbled the steering wheel. The car skidded left, right, and left again. The tires squealed and left long black marks on the asphalt. Encouraged by her success, Ariel maneuvered the shift-lever and slammed the vehicle out of Drive and into Park. There came an awful rending sound, and the vehicle thudded. Shuddering, it finally came to a stop.

A moment later, the door opened, and the man popped out. "Listen, sweetheart," he called out.

Ariel was surprised by his jovial tone. She'd expected something sinister, cruel even, and brimming with spite and anger. This man was grinning like a jester and looked like he was having the time of his life.

"If you think it's that easy, you better think again."

He had a gun.

Ariel stretched out her hands. Stopping teeny, tiny flying projectiles going at ridiculously fast speeds was not her forte. She had practiced it with guns aimed away from her with some success, but never directed at her. Ariel paused, confused, and tried to latch onto the bullet, but the air was empty. Panic bubbled in her throat. She'd somehow missed—

Stinging pain blossomed on her hip. Ariel looked down. A wide, bright splotch of purple painted her hip. "Paint gun?" she said out loud, disbelieving. Of course, the bullet hadn't been where she'd expected. Paint rounds traveled so much more slowly.

"You got it, gorgeous," the man said again. "Much more effective. And way more fun." He vaulted over the hood of one of the stalled cars he'd crashed into earlier and tackled Ariel.

In defense, Ariel shot up into the air. "Get off me!" she yelled. He had her in a tight hug, and it was definitely a frightening position to be in. Even if he did smell like some amazing aftershave. "Let go! Buster, you are going to be so sorry!"

"Max," he said, his voice purring in her ear. "Please

call me Max. And if I let go, I'll fall. You don't really want me to fall, do you?" He shifted his grip around her and instead of being vise-like, it was suddenly intimate. She could feel his hands on her shoulders and splayed against her ribs, warm and broad. Face to face now, Ariel stared into his eyes. They were green, like the darkest pine needles in a shaded forest.

A spark of indignance flared through her. She was not here to gaze into the eyes of a reprobate. Nor to think poetic thoughts about his debonair attractiveness. She was here to rescue people hurt by his miscreant deeds, and she needed to put a stop to his continuing to hurt more people. "Listen, *buster*," she emphasized the incorrect name. She would not start calling him Max. Not even if he did look like a very handsome Max. "This little tirade of yours is over."

Max laughed. "Of course it is, sweet pea." He glanced down. "If you haven't noticed yet, you've got us so high up, everyone looks like ants." His grip around her tightened, but it felt more like an amorous embrace than a man clutching for dear life so he wouldn't fall to his death. "I like it," he said, his already deep voice husk-toned and full of promising intentions. "It's nice being up here all alone with you." He leaned in slowly, his eyes closed and his lush lips pouted out into an obvious moue.

Ariel gaped. She'd rocketed them sky-high, and Max's reaction was to try and kiss her? Her first thought was to drop him and see how much he enjoyed a one-way trip, but she couldn't kill him. Not even if she wanted to just a little. What she wanted more was to let him kiss her. "You're a criminal," she pointed out, trying to forestall his actions, "and obviously a thief if you think you can steal a kiss."

One eye popped open and both eyebrows rose, giving him a squinty, affronted look. It seemed put on, though, and disingenuous. Beneath it, he was highly amused. "Sweetheart, I don't steal kisses. I bestow them. Completely and utterly different." He closed the one eye, and his expression smoothed out. He leaned in again, much more quickly, and caught Ariel straight on where her face shield didn't cover her mouth.

Max's hand on her shoulder shifted to cradle the back of her neck, and he immediately deepened the kiss. There was the barest scratch from his clean-shaven face against her skin. The scent of his aftershave enveloped her, causing a plunge in her stomach entirely unrelated to the short plummeting dip they'd taken when their lips had met and she'd briefly lost focus and forgotten they were flying.

His lips were soft against hers, and he kissed like he was a man in love, not overwhelming, not demanding, not insistent. In his arms, she felt cherished, as if the kiss itself were the end and the beginning, and all meaningful things in between. She melted against him, accepting the benefaction. Then, at the end, the tempo changed, and he pressed a little harder against her. Devotion, yes, but also adoration and more than a hint of lust. He desired her, and he wanted her to know it.

Heat seared Ariel's insides as the fantasy of taking

him to bed welled up. She wanted so much more, she practically burned with the urges developing within. His kiss faded as he left her mouth and rubbed against her chin to trail down her throat, ending with an embellishing swirl across the jut of her collarbone. Ariel gasped in air and enjoyed the final sensation as it permeated to her very core. Torrents and eddies of desire coursed through her. The cascade of bright need and possessiveness felt nearly physical, and Ariel flexed her fingers, trying to dispel it.

A barrage of small explosions startled them both. For a moment, Max's face registered real concern and confusion.

Ariel caught her breath as she bewilderedly tried to make sense of the noise and small concussions. "What just happened?" she asked, still recovering her senses.

Suave attitude immediately restored, Max nipped briefly at Ariel's mouth. "I just kissed the daylights out of you. And you caused all my paintballs to self implode."

"What?" Ariel tried to grasp his meaning, but it was slow to sink in.

"I have to admit, it was an excellent, excellent kiss. Worth every single paintball." Max motioned with his head to his pockets and to the paint-gun slung across his back with a band. Everything was dripping virulent green, purple, yellow, and red. A moment passed. The wet paint had saturated the fabric of his jacket and was now oozing outward. "Best course of action is always to wash it as soon as possible. I have a great recipe for a prewash soak that I can share with you. It uses detergent and ammonia."

"You do that," Ariel said, finally recovering her senses. It had been a fantastic kiss, but the exploding paintballs reminded her Max had been smashing up cars and hurting people. Kissing him again was a bad idea, and taking him to bed was out of the question. He obviously kissed women indiscriminately, and he was probably full of germs. Rakishly handsome or not, he was full to the brim of trouble and more trouble. "I'm still handing you over to the police, buster."

Max raised a single eyebrow. "Do tell." He looked down. "What police?"

Ariel reoriented herself and realized with dismay that he'd distracted her entirely. They gone even higher than before and kept moving. The bridge was long gone, and they were floating over the very edge of where the suburbs turned into farmland.

"How about you set me down, and we call it a day?" Max offered.

Ariel scowled. "No. I'll have us back in a jiffy. Hold on."

"With pleasure, *mademoiselle*." He shifted his arms around her again, until their position reflected that of dancers. One strong hand pressed into the small of her back and the other arm wrapped around her shoulders.

Ariel chose to ignore him. As long as he didn't touch anything he wasn't supposed to, she wouldn't drop him smack in the center of the closest duck pond.

The flight back only took a minute. Even with the extra weight, Ariel was well practiced at using her flying abilities. The police were still at the bridge, although they appeared uncertain if they needed to continue to maintain the blockade or not. Several ambulances were there as well, their spinning lights flashing on all the damaged vehicles. The sight sent a pang of agitation through her. She shouldn't have been dilly-dallying up in the sky kissing the bad guy. She needed to stay focused. She wasn't even supposed to be fighting. Her goal had always been to assist with rescue operations. Maybe Velda was right. Even if she did have these incredible powers, perhaps she was better off using them in smaller ways to do good and help people.

Or maybe she needed to stop equivocating and accept the fact that she needed to learn how to handle herself in a confrontation.

"You sure you want to turn me over to these knuckle-draggers?" Max asked as they got closer. "I know a little hideaway. We could get cozy."

"Tempting," Ariel said as she decreased their altitude. "Maybe give me a call when you give up your life of crime. And get out of jail." She didn't give him the dignity of lowering him all the way to the ground. She hovered about five feet up. "Jump."

He gave her another grin. "I look forward to crossing swords with you again."

As soon as he released her, she missed the warmth of his body pressed against hers.

He dropped gracefully out of her arms and landed safely, going down to one knee to absorb the impact. From the ground, he blew her a kiss. "I'll see you soon, sweetheart." His words didn't sound like a threat, more like a yearning promise.

Police swarmed him a moment later.

"Thanks, miss," said one of the nearby officers. "Any chance you'd like to come down and explain things?"

Ariel considered it. She'd been meaning to have a long chat with the police at some point. Shorter encounters had at least convinced them she wasn't the enemy and was only there to assist. The first few times they'd been on the verge of deciding to forcibly interview her—although interview was just a friendlier term for capture—except she hadn't done anything more questionable than evacuate children from a burning building. "Some other day." She looked at all the damage. "It looks like there's still work to do."

The officer didn't look pleased, but he didn't move to restrain her.

Of course, she was still floating above his head, so it would have been terribly ineffective. Ariel caught a last glimpse of Max as the police stuffed him into one of their cruisers. A quiet sadness enveloped her for a moment. She'd liked him. Even though he was a deplorable criminal, he had charm and wit. Plus, he'd kissed the daylights out of her, and she desperately wanted more.

Resolutely, Ariel turned back to the scene of destruction. Tow trucks were arriving to take away the demolished, disabled vehicles. She touched down near one of the ambulances. "Can I be of any assistance?" she asked.

Two paramedics and a fireman stared. They had cups of coffee in their hands and had been chatting.

"Uh, thanks, but not really," said the female paramedic. She was blonde and looked to be in her fifties. She also looked incredibly poised and confident. "It actually looks worse than it is. All those smashed-up cars and not a single person needed to go to the hospital. The worst thing we had was a bloody nose, and we got it stopped in a couple minutes."

Ariel blinked in surprise. "Seriously?" She glanced back at the ruinous scene.

"Seriously," the woman said. "Kind of amazing, isn't it? Unbelievable, but true."

"And a scraped elbow," added in the other paramedic, a younger man with a square face. "That did need a bandage."

"Nothing even caught on fire," said the fireman. "It's a demolition derby out there."

"Oh. Okay." Ariel turned to go. Her main mission had been to assist people, and there wasn't a single person who required it. She felt very out of sorts.

"Hey, miss—"

Ariel looked back. "Yes?"

"Who are you? How do you—"

"Fly?" Ariel supplied.

"Yeah. How?" the woman asked. All three of them looked intently interested. "It's fantastic."

"I don't know. I just can. Bye." Ariel waggled her fingers in a wave and took to the air again, leaving them to stare. She went up high enough to get a good look at the entire scene. It seemed impossible there hadn't been any serious injuries. There had certainly been a lot of damage. She spent a moment to consider the armored truck. The doors were open and nothing was inside it, but enough time had elapsed for the police to have removed whatever Max had been carrying. She wondered what it had been. She'd assumed money. But maybe she'd been too quick to jump to conclusions. He had been creating a lot of chaos and damage. But maybe the better question was why.

Deciding the authorities had things well covered and she wasn't exactly needed anymore, Ariel left. She retrieved her backpack off the roof of the café and headed home. The whole thing hadn't taken more than an hour. It seemed like she'd been out there for days, but she still had the entire afternoon ahead.

She landed on the roof of the apartment building where she and Velda lived. In their last year of college, it was cheaper to live off campus. They had the top apartment, which meant it was easy to come and go from the roof without being seen.

Ariel exited from the roof into their kitchen. A bunch of bananas sat on the counter, and Ariel could hear the television on in the next room. She snagged a banana and wandered into the living room. Velda was there and the news was on.

Velda looked relieved. "He got away," she said. She did a double take. "And you're purple."

"He shot me with a paint gun." Ariel dropped into

the closest chair. She peeled her banana and took a bite while she watched the television. The attack was all over the news. Footage of the bridge came courtesy of a news helicopter and a scrolling banner across the bottom announced the previously captured criminal had made his escape prior to being delivered to the station. Luckily, no officers had been hurt.

"What happened up there?" Velda asked. Behind her glasses, her eyes were huge.

Ariel blushed and gave Velda a well-edited version of the whole adventure. "What do you think he wanted?" Ariel asked. She finished her banana and dropped the peel into the waste bin.

Velda rolled her eyes. "To ask you out on a date." She moved over to Ariel. "Want me to take care of that?" She pointed to the large purple splotch.

"Please," Ariel said. She watched as Velda rubbed her fingers across the coloration. The purple paint peeled away as if it had never been attached. Velda's particular ability was to unlock things. A door or a pass code didn't exist that could stand against her. Dirt, grease, and grime also unlocked their grip from fibers at her command. It was a much more understated ability, but if Velda ever honed it, she would be far more powerful than Ariel.

"There. All set." Velda chucked the rubbery paint after the banana peel. She perched on the arm of Ariel's chair. "Do you think he might be one of us? That's a whole lot of luck to not hurt anyone in the process. It'd make more sense if he had some kind of ability and was controlling the outcome."

Ariel's attention drifted back to the television. "And a whole lot of distraction. I keep wondering if he was diverting attention from something else. Something much bigger." The thought was intriguing and made a lot of sense. She wondered if he'd plotted and planned for good or for ill. "As for the other...." Ariel touched her fingers to her lips, remembering the extraordinary kiss and Max's uncanny farewell promise to see her soon. She looked forward to the encounter. "I'll ask him the next time I see him."

Glass Slippers, Hardly Worn

Bibi Rizer

ASHEL TUGGED AT the bindings on her hands, and nearly turned an ankle as the highwayman led her away from the carriage and into the dark forest. After everything she'd been through that day, it would be just her luck to be kidnapped on the way to the ball and forced to tramp through the wild in the most uncomfortable pair of shoes ever conceived of.

"My family won't stand for this," she said, more because she felt the declaration necessary than because it was actually true. "My footmen will free themselves and come after us. I expect them at any moment."

"Your footmen? Miss, when I tried to speak to one of them, he squeaked. Your coachman mewed like a kitten." The highwayman's voice was as deep and mysterious as the forest that now rose all around them.

Ashel trembled at the sound of it.

"At any rate, my men will keep close watch over them. I am confident we won't be followed."

He helped her step over a fallen log, their way lit only by the moon and the stars peeking through the heavy canopy above. His strong grip burned through the silk of her new gown, and when she stepped down from the log, he momentarily put his arm around her, protectively.

She wasn't frightened exactly. The stories of young ladies being carried off by highwaymen nearly always ended in the ladies in question being robbed of their honor; since Ashel had no honor to lose, she felt strangely calm about this possibility. Her beloved father, her inheritance, her station in life, and yes, her honor were all long gone. What more had she to lose?

As she trudged through the dark, the highwayman's strong grip on her never loosening, Ashel thought of honor, and the sweet-natured stable boy, Hobby, who had relieved her of hers over five years past. Only her late father's horse master knew of this horrifying transgression. Ashel's begging had saved the boy from the gallows, but nothing could save their love. He had disappeared in the night, and the horse master had concocted a story about his joining the King's army. Then a tense month had passed while Ashel actually wished she might be with his child, but that was not to be. Hobby was never seen again.

He had been an awkward boy, his head perpetually shaved by the cruel horse master who had a paranoia about fleas and lice, his nose often peeling from sunburn, his underfed frame gangly and thin. But Ashel had loved him just the same. Loved his gentle ways, his laughter, his kisses, the multitude of loving nicknames he gave her: Ashputtle, The Queen of Hearths, and her favorite, Ashelina. She had loved giving herself to him that fateful night, their naked bodies wound together in the hayloft.

Hobby had cupped her small breasts reverently, pinched her aching nipples, and cried her name as he spent his seed inside her. Then he cradled her and kissed and licked away the stinging that her deflowering had left. It had been his first time too; how he knew what to do so expertly, making her moan and writhe under his tongue, she never found out. She had no complaints though. Until the master had burst in on them, The encounter had been like a dream. But then, like a dream, her darling Hob was gone.

Ashel had swallowed her sadness as her stepsisters teased her about Hobby. "Oh do you miss the little horse boy? Do you miss his smell? I could make a sachet of manure for you to put under your pillow." And in her dusty little corner of the woodshed, she had dreamed of Hobby's hands and other parts of him that were not so *little*. And she had chafed at the unfairness of it. To be treated like a servant in her father's house, yet denied the pleasure of love, maybe even a marriage, with another servant because that was beneath the daughter of a nobleman, even a dead one. In between their mooning over the king's insipid son, she endured merciless teasing from her stepsisters about that, too. "Who would marry someone who smells like a tinder box? You'll die with your dusty little hole unpoked, Ash-pot."

If only they knew what a magnificent poking Hobby had given her that night. Sometimes Ashel smiled to remember it, despite her stepsisters' cruel words.

Then one day, fed up with their years of mockery, Ashel had decided she would marry their feckless fop of a prince just to spite them. A silly impulse from a silly young girl she now realized, and she chided herself for wasting her meager savings on the scheme. If she hadn't worked that witch's spell—that she had paid handsomely for, too—and called up that ridiculous fairy with her pink cloud of magic and lace, she wouldn't be in this predicament. Festooned in gaudy jewels, dragging a heavy silk gown through brambles and thorns, gasping from a corset that was almost all bone, and her feet! Slippers made of glass! It was not to be borne.

"Wait," Ashel finally said. "These infernal shoes. Let me take them off. I beg you."

The highwayman's eyes twinkled below the rim of his black hat. "How will you walk without shoes? The ground is rough and thick with bristles and pine barbs."

Did he smile under his scarf? Ashel attempted to cross her arms, stubbornly, a gesture she had seldom made since her father's death. But of course with her hands bound in front of her, the effect was more comical than stubborn. The highwayman actually laughed, a low grumbling laugh that evoked something warm in Ashel's heart. The sound reminded her of the purring of a barn cat.

"Perhaps if you tell me where we are going," Ashel said. "And how far away it is, I can imagine if I might bear it. My feet are not delicate lady's feet, despite what you may think."

"I have a better idea." The highwayman lifted her

easily into his arms and, cradling her, continued through the trees.

Ashel was inclined to struggle and protest at first, but something about the highwayman made her feel oddly safe. She lay her head against the coarse wool of his cloak and, with her next breath, inhaled the warm familiar scent of someone who lived in close company with horses. Straw, horse sweat, and faintly, but not unpleasantly, manure. Either this was a stolen cloak or the highwayman was a horseman. Again Ashel thought of Hobby then and blinked back a tear. This was not the time to show weakness. Though she was increasingly resigned to her fate, she planned to be at least somewhat in control too.

"Why did you not take my horses?" Ashel said. "If you're a rider as I suspect you are, could you and your men not use fine horses like them?"

The highwayman let out another low rumbling laugh. "Fine horses? One had whiskers, the other scales. I recognize enchantments when I see them, lady. Those are no more horses than I am a prince."

That made Ashel think of the ball she was missing, and all the fine food and drink that might be found there. Her stomach rumbled at the thought. "Well then, are you not afraid I will enchant you too? Maybe turn you into a mouse and myself an owl to eat you?"

"I might enjoy being eaten by you, lady,"

To her horror, Ashel laughed. And such a vulgar image popped into her head that she felt her whole body flush with heat and embarrassment.

"You have a lovely laugh," the highwayman said. "I hope I can make you laugh again."

Ashel wasn't of a mood to indulge him. She pressed her lips together and thought of tragic things until the urge to giggle subsided. "I regret to share this news with you," she finally said. "But my jewels are enchanted too. At midnight, they will turn into pumpkin seeds and peppercorns."

"Is that so?" He didn't sound very concerned.

"Yes. So unless you plan on selling the jewels before midnight, I offer little worth to you."

They stopped in a clearing, the bright moon high in the dark sky above them. The highwayman tilted his head down and gazed into Ashel's eyes with an intensity she felt to her core. The corset dug into her as she gasped, her hard nipples pressing painfully into the stiff linen.

"You have great worth to me, lady," he said.

With one hand still holding her, he threw down his satchel and loosened his cloak, shaking it out and laying it on the bed of moss and pine needles at his feet. Then he gently set her down.

Her feet in the glass shoes sank into the soft ground beneath the cloak.

The highwayman knelt, carefully removed first one torturous shoe, and then the other. He set them on a nearby log, where they twinkled in the moonlight. "Are those enchanted too?"

Ashel regarded the hateful shoes with scorn. "No. You may feel free to sell those whenever you please.

They were forged by a witless glassblower, the son of the witch whose spell I bought. He thought if I wore them to the ball every woman in the kingdom would suddenly want a pair. Thought they looked lovely on my feet, even though he made them a size too small."

The highwayman tugged Ashel's hands until she sat across from him. "You do have lovely feet, lady. May I?" He took one foot and began rubbing away the pain and ache.

Would he ask permission for everything he took from her? That didn't seem very highwayman-like. What kind of rogue was this? Just her luck to meet a rascal who was too polite to ravish her. But his hands on her feet, which were sore not just from the glass shoes but from the hours she spent sweeping and cooking and washing and dusting, were sheer heaven. She let herself fall back on the cloak and sighed with pleasure as the muscles of her feet and ankles softened and warmed.

When she felt his lips on the top of her foot, Ashel almost pulled away. If she resisted, would he stop? If he didn't stop, would that ruin things? She suspected it would. But she hadn't been touched by a man since Hobby, and what better way to ease her needs than with a scoundrel in the dark woods? No one would know. If he let her live, she could walk back to her home and visit the witch again tomorrow for a spell against his seed. Her life would continue as normal, not changed but for the two years' worth of coin she had wasted on her idle fancy about the prince's ball. Paying the witch again would gall, but getting with child by a highwayman would ruin her just as easily as by a stable boy.

Ashel sighed again as the highwayman's lips travelled slowly up her calf, pushing the ruffled dress out of the way. When he reached her knee, she became self-conscious of the bruises that hours of scrubbing the hearth had left. But the highwayman only nibbled there lightly, trailing his fingers over her skin. She looked down to see he had untied the scarf from his face and removed his hat. In the fading moonlight, she could barely see him but for long thick curls of dark hair and those dark eyes under heavy brows. There was a seriousness in his expression as he looked up at her from where he crouched by her knee, though his lips were curled into a smile.

Well, he's handsome anyway, Ashel thought, *and strong. And his lips are so…ahhhh…soft.* She longed to feel them in more intimate areas, longed to feel those curls of hair tickling places other than her knee.

"Do you want me to untie you?" he asked when his kisses reached the middle of her thigh. The offer certainly suggested Ashel was not quite a prisoner. But something was also intriguing about the idea of being ravished while bound at the wrists. She shook her head.

The highwayman smiled wickedly.

Perhaps he was intrigued by the idea, too.

He slid his hand up the inside of her thighs, spreading her knees apart, not exactly roughly, but not gently either.

Ashel flinched at his sudden boldness and the twinge of pain in her hips.

The highwayman sprung back, kneeling back on his heels and looking down on her. "Forgive me." Remorse glinted in his eyes, so genuine, so warm. "Did I hurt you?" He reached out, tentative, and softly caressed her thighs.

Her heart awoke for the first time since she had steeled it in the months after Hobby's departure. "No. You just startled me, that's all. I…I wonder if I could know your name. I mean if this is to be, should we not know each other's names?"

Smiling, he leaned forward and rested a hand on either side of her hips.

As his dark silhouette loomed over her, Ashel silently noted how large he was compared to her. Instead of feeling threatened however, she felt protected. And excited. She wondered if he was large…everywhere.

"Hawk is my name, lady. And you are?"

"Ashel," she stammered. "Ashel Adelsmann. The daughter of the late Lord Adelsmann."

His breath swirled in the shell of her ear, and his nose brushed the sensitive skin along her jaw. "Ashel is a beautiful name."

She turned her head, and he captured her lips.

Hawk's kisses were as soft as they had been on her feet and legs. She parted her lips to welcome him. He eagerly darted his tongue into her mouth and let it linger there, caressing hers with practiced strokes. The corset dug into her as her breathing quickened. As Hawk lowered his body onto hers, she shivered, feeling her sex clench with anticipation. His firm manhood pressed into her thigh, even through the layers of petticoats and bloomers. Shamelessly, she opened her legs and tried to draw him closer to the position she desired, to press on her awakening flower, but the reams of silk and cotton impeded her.

Hawk seemed to sense her discomfort, and he leaned back once again. "Is something wrong?"

"Yes." She plucked at her bodice. "I hate this gown. I had no idea that ladies must be so uncomfortable. I know it will turn back into my simple homespun at midnight, but I don't think I can wait that long."

"Well." Hawk trailed a finger across the bodice of her dress. "It would be my pleasure to remove it." He tried first opening some buttons, but found them only decorative. Looking for ties proved equally fruitless. Then he tried lifting it over her shoulders, but it wouldn't budge past the tightly fitted waist. "Good heavens, woman, were you sewn into this?"

"It's enchanted, sir. What did you expect?"

"Must another enchantment remove it? I'm afraid my gown-removing skills are limited to the worldly arts."

Ashel chuckled. "I expect a knife will serve. Do be careful though."

Hawk reached for a scabbard on his belt. A small blade flashed in the starlight, and Ashel held her breath as he began at the hem of her dress. With raw ripping sounds, he sliced through the silk and cotton lining and soon the whole monstrous affair was lying open around her, like a filleted fish.

Hawk then carefully slit each sleeve from neckline to

wrist, so he didn't have to untie her.

When the heavy folds of fabric fell away, Ashel sat among them in her shift and corset, like a mermaid cut from the belly of a whale. The night's chill washed over her. She felt suddenly exposed, and had she been able to, she might have hugged herself.

But with her hands still bound, that action was impossible. Instead, she watched Hawk unbutton his doublet and slip it off. Ashel strained her eyes in the dark, biting her lip as he untucked and removed his tunic, before unbuckling his belt and tossing it aside, along with his knife and flintlock pistol.

In the dim shadows of the trees, she could see enough of his body to know that whatever thievery he did, it was hard work that kept him muscled and strong. For the first time, she wanted to be unbound so she could run her hands over his hard stomach, trail her fingers through the line of dark hair above his navel and up across his chest.

But before she gathered her wits enough to ask, he pulled up her bound hands and pinned them above her head. "There," he said. "You look lovely like that. Lovely and fuckable, if I may say so."

"Oh…" Ashel said with a gasp.

Hawk didn't wait for her to say more. He laid his free hand on the side of her face and held her there while he kissed her, his lips and tongue hungry. Then that hand slid down over her neck, from her collarbone to the swell of her breasts barely contained in the tightly laced corset.

"You can cut that off too, if you want to," Ashel said, breathlessly.

It was Hawk's turn to chuckle. "Oh, I don't think so." He grabbed the front of her shift and corset and pulled them down roughly, just enough that her nipples peeked over the boning and cotton. "Ah… that's glorious. Your breasts are everything I…" His voice trailed off for a moment, as though distracted. "Imagined. I've been imagining them since we met on the road." He took one nipple then the other between his teeth, biting just to edge of pain.

Her body opened and warmed, coming to life for the first time in years.

With one nipple still in his mouth, Hawk reached under her shift to the fine cotton bloomers. Another tearing sounded, and something ragged and white went sailing through the air. Then his fingers were on her, stroking her cleft, dipping into her hungry opening with one finger, then two.

When a third joined them, Ashel made a strangled sound, but Hawk never faltered. Ashel felt the mix of pleasure and pressure almost too much to bear.

He bit down on her nipple again as his fingers stroked in and out of her wet tunnel, stretching her, opening her, awakening parts of her long dormant. As another moan cut through the night, Hawk moved his head up and stilled her noises, kissing her, the tenderness of his lips contrasting with the relentlessness of his powerful fingers.

"Hawk…" Ashel said against his mouth, a desperate

hunger rising inside. It wasn't enough. His hand would never be enough. She wanted all of him. "Take me, please."

He removed his fingers abruptly, leaving her bereft and empty, but in seconds, he had tugged down the front of his trousers, freeing his broad manhood to spring out and bounce heavily against Ashel's thighs. As she gasped at his intimidating size, Hawk shoved the hem of her shift out of the way and for a second, Ashel felt the cold night air on her exposed wet nest. But it was fleeting, for Hawk lay on her, covering her again with his warm body, pushing her legs farther apart with his hips. Then while one hand still held hers pinned over her head, his other guided his hard rod to her opening, pushing inside.

She whimpered with the pressure, sure with every inch he advanced that she could take no more. But he was persistent, as though some force drew him deeper into her, to the parts she had thought closed forever. But they opened for him, bit by bit, inch by ecstatic inch. Soon he was fully seated inside her, the stretching sting receding into a delicious fullness.

"Yes..." she said, as he began to move. "Oh yesssss..." She rocked her hips under him, matching him thrust for thrust.

Hawk released her hands, and propping himself on one elbow, he looked down on her face as he slid his free hand between them. He found her button of pleasure that had so long been neglected, sliding his fingers into her juices.

Ashel's body trembled as he stroked and fucked her,

holding her bound hands firmly pinned above her head.

"Your cunny is tight," Hawk panted. "Like a glove made just for me. So tight and hot." His fingers slackened and released her wrists.

She lifted her bound hands over his head and tangled her fingers in his damp hair, pulling his face down to kiss her. Her legs wrapped around his buttocks; she pressed her heels down on him as he thrust, deeper and deeper into her arousal. He moaned then and kissed her with more hunger and urgency, his lips, tongue, and teeth sucking, lashing at her, biting. Their rhythm intensified; Hawk's pounding reached a part of her that had never been touched. Pausing briefly from working his fingers on her slit, Hawk suddenly pushed her legs up, propping them over his broad shoulders.

The position was coarse, debauched even, and perfect. As he rose, the angle of fucking changed, his swollen cock sliding over uncharted landscapes of pleasure and exquisite pain. Ashel cried out, overwhelmed by Hawk moving, thrusting against some secret place inside her. "Hawk, Hawk…I'm going to come. Touch me again…"

He obeyed without hesitation. Snaking one hand back over her mound, he slipped a single finger against her slit and pressed on the spot there that set off paroxysms of pleasure.

She had so longed for this. A glorious tingling thrill began in her toes. It shot up her legs and, gathering strength at the point of their union, exploded throughout her body like a great flame, leaving her crying out and gasping for breath.

Rather than take a moment to let her compose herself, Hawk kept moving, even increasing the intensity of his thrusts, continuing to stroke his thumb over her slit as she writhed and whimpered beneath him. The sensations were too much; she was moments away from begging him to stop when he whisked his hand away from her aching pearl and clutched at her round bottom, pressing himself so deeply into her she felt it in her womb. No witch's spell to defeat his seed. She wanted his child. She wanted him forever, and to hell with the consequences.

"Ashel...Ashel...," Hawk chanted her name with every thrust. He lowered down onto one elbow, pushing her knees farther back, and roughly fisted a handful of her hair, pulling it, the sharpness focusing her pleasure once more. "I've dreamt of this...dreamt of you so long..."

Her cunny spasmed again, shooting bursts of lightning through her like a great storm.

As he came, he pressed his mouth on hers, shuddering, gasping her name against her lips one more time. "*Ashelina...*"

Ashel had never thought it possible to die from happiness and ecstasy, but in that second, it seemed not only possible, but likely.

After a moment, he moved in the dark, carefully lifting her legs from his shoulders, stroking them softly, as he laid them back on the cloak beneath them.

Ashel gasped as he pulled out of her bruised and

swollen cunny. When she saw the knife flash, she lifted her hands.

Hawk carefully sliced through the thin rope bindings.

Ashel lowered her hands to run them over his stubbled face and through his sweat-dripping curls. "Who would have guessed you would grow such a beautiful mane of hair, Hobby?"

He drew a sharp breath then kissed her, tenderly, running a hand over her exposed nipples, before lovingly tucking them back under her shift and corset. "When did you know?"

"The moment I felt your cock pressing on my thigh I suspected." Ashel felt her eyes fill with tears and tried to cover it with a laugh. Her lost love was not to be fooled. He stroked her face, brushing hair from her eyes and wiped away her tears as she went on. "I didn't dare dream it could be true, but who else in the kingdom could be so endowed?" She let her hands trail down his shoulders, over his muscular back, and his thick powerful arms. "And how the rest of you has grown to fit your natural blessings. Were you a soldier, after all?"

"Of fortune. I fought for a time, for the enemy of our king. To regain the stolen territory in the north. But the rewards were not great." He leaned forward and whispered wickedly in her ear, "So I became a thief."

"Of hearts, no doubt."

"Never, my love. I waited for you these long years. Waited until I had grown and changed enough that no one would recognize me. My former master assured me he would have me flogged and burned alive if ever I showed my pimply face on your father's estate."

Ashel rolled onto her side as Hawk lay beside her.

He gathered her in his arms, tucking her head onto his shoulder.

"How young we both were then," she said, twisting a lock of his hair around her finger. "How did you know I'd be on the road tonight?"

Hawk smiled.

She could just see his teeth flash in the dark.

"I bestowed some coin on the witch, too. She's had a very good week."

Ashel eyed the sliced-open gown beneath them. The garment had transformed back to a simple homespun dress. She felt the jewels at her neck—now only seeds on a length of cotton thread. And back on the road, she knew, was a pumpkin, a kitten, a rat, a lizard, and two very confused mice. "Midnight has passed."

"And here you are, still a princess, my lady," Hawk said. "Would you deign to be the princess of thieves? I'm afraid it will be a principality of two. The men I had with me will have slithered away at midnight, too. Back into the nest of snakes from whence they came." He kissed her again.

Ashel's heart soared. To have her beautiful boy Hob back in her arms was superior to a legion of loyal subjects, to a world of them. "An alliance between the Queen of Hearths and the Prince of Thieves?" she said. "How strong we would be. Who could defeat us?"

"Certainly not a poxy horse master."

"Or two hideous stepsisters. I wonder which one got

her talons into our hapless princeling? I almost feel sorry for him."

"But not really."

"No."

They kissed and held each other, whispering plans to pilfer Ashel's favorite stallion from under the cruel horse master's nose. Hawk dug a clean tunic from his satchel, and by wrapping the remains of Ashel's dress around her like a kilt, they fashioned attire suitable for the journey back to her father's estate.

As Hawk made to lift her, to carry her back to the road, Ashel stopped him, pointing to the glass slippers, still twinkling on the log. "What of those?" she said. "What will we do with them?"

Hawk gathered them up, wrapped them in his scarf, and tucked them carefully into his satchel. "What good thieves do with all pretty but impractical things. Sell them to someone who knows no better."

He held out his arms, and Ashel leapt into them. He carried her out of the forest and along the long road back to her father's house, where Ashel helped herself to a change of clothes and, more importantly, a comfortable pair of boots. After tiptoeing past the snoring horse master, they were soon riding Ashel's favorite stallion into the pink glow of the rising sun.

They lived thievishly ever after.

About the Authors

Axa Lee is an erotica-writing farm girl who grazes cattle in her yard and herds incorrigible poultry with a cowardly dog. Her work appears in several anthologies. Her partner is finally getting used to answering weird rhetorical questions that begin with the disclaimer, "So this is for a story…"
menagegeek.blogspot.com | twitter.com/axalee1

Bibi Rizer is a writer and blogger who lives in Vancouver, Canada. When she's not writing sexy stories, she designs book covers featuring sexy vampires, trolls, millionaires, and lifeguards. If you enjoyed her story, she has several more available.
bibirizer.com | bibirizer.com/news | facebook.com/pages/Bibi-Rizer/845707895448516

Cela Winter took up writing after a career as a restaurant chef. Really. She has several works of erotic fiction in print and online. She lives on the fringes of Portland, Oregon, where she is working on a novel—when the Muse isn't distracting her with short story ideas.
celawinter.com |amazon.com/author/celawinter | facebook.com/celaserotica

Cynthia Young writes tantalizing, passionate romances set during the Regency era. She enjoys writing stories with strong characters that triumph over challenges to achieve their happily-ever-after. Cynthia lives in the Pacific Northwest where the rain and numerous coffee houses make the perfect writing companions.

cynthiayoungauthor.com | cynthiayoungauthor.com/news | facebook.com/CynthiaYoungAuthor

Delilah Night is a native New Englander who now calls steamy Southeast Asia home. Check out her first novella, *Capturing the Moment*, a sizzling erotic romance set in Siem Reap, Cambodia. Delilah's deliciously naughty short stories can be found in more than a dozen anthologies.

delilahnight.com | twitter.com/Delilah_Night | facebook.com/DelilahNight

Elle James spent twenty years livin' and lovin' in South Texas, ranching horses, cattle, goats, ostriches, and emus. A former IT professional, Elle happily writes full-time, penning adventures that keep her readers begging for more. When she's not writing, she's traveling, snow-skiing, boating, or riding her ATV, concocting new stories.

ellejames.com | facebook.com/ellejamesauthor | ellejames.com/ElleContact.htm

Emma Jay has been writing romance for decades, using her string of celebrity crushes as inspiration for her heroes. Writing romance is like falling in love, over and over again. Creating characters and love stories is an addiction she has no intention of breaking.

emmajayromance.com | facebook.com/EmmaJayRomanceAuthor | twitter.com/EmmaJayromance

Erzabet Bishop is an award winning and bestselling author of erotic and paranormal romance. She lives in Houston, Texas, and when she isn't writing about sexy shifters or voluptuous heroines, she enjoys playing in local bookstores and watching movies with her husband and furry kids.

erzabetwrites.wix.com/erzabetbishop | erzabetsenchantments.blogspot.com | facebook.com/erzabetbishopauthor

Jennifer Kacey is a writer, mother, and business owner in the great state of Texas. She sings in the shower, plays piano in her dreams, and has to have a different color of nail polish every week. Best advice she's ever been given? Find the real you and never settle for anything less.

jenniferkacey.com | twitter.com/JenniferKacey | facebook.com/jennifer.kacey.7

Megan Mitcham is a *USA Today* bestselling author who pens sizzling suspense novels that whisk you across the globe, wedge your heart in your throat, make your hands sweat and your naughty bits tingle. Check out her special forces heroes in the Base Branch Series.

meganmitcham.com | meganmitcham.com/subscribe-library.html | facebook.com/AuthorMeganMitcham

Mia Hopkins writes lush romances starring fun, sexy characters who love to get down and dirty. She's a sucker for working class heroes, brainy heroines, and wisecracking best friends. Thirsty for hot cowboys? Be sure to check out her Cowboy Cocktail series.

miahopkinsauthor.com/p/welcome.html |
twitter.com/MiaHopkinsxoxo |
facebook.com/Mia-Hopkins-Books-1415093612075704

T.G. Haynes is a British writer whose background is in local radio. Since the publication of his debut erotic novel, *Pleasure Island*, he has turned his attention to writing a series of breath-taking, racy short stories. His second novel, *Dream World*, has recently been released.

goodreads.com/author/show/8351481.T_G_Haynes

Tray Ellis is a writer and leisure time gardener who loves to spin imaginary adventures and heartfelt romances. Her short stories can be found in anthologies and as stand-alones. Check out her social media for links and free reads.

twitter.com/TrayEllisWrites | trayellis.blogspot.com |
facebook.com/tray.ellis.54

About The Editor

Delilah Devlin is a *New York Times* and *USA Today* bestselling author of erotica and erotic romance. She has published over a hundred sixty erotic stories in multiple genres and lengths, and is published by Atria/Strebor, Avon, Berkley, Black Lace, Cleis Press, Ellora's Cave, Grand Central, Harlequin Spice, HarperCollins: Mischief, Kensington, Kindle, Kindle Worlds, Montlake, Running Press, and Samhain Publishing.

Her short stories have appeared in multiple Cleis Press collections, including *Lesbian Cowboys, Girl Crush, Fairy Tale Lust, Lesbian Lust, Passion, Lesbian Cops, Dream Lover, Carnal Machines, Best Erotic Romance (2012), Suite Encounters, Girl Fever, Girls Who Score, Duty and Desire* and *Best Lesbian Romance of 2013*. For Cleis Press, she edited *Girls Who Bite, She Shifters, Cowboy Lust, Smokin' Hot Firemen, High Octane Heroes, Cowboy Heat,* and *Hot Highlanders and Wild Warriors*. She also edited *Conquests: An Anthology of Smoldering Viking Romance*.

delilahdevlin.com | facebook.com/DelilahDevlinFanPage | twitter.com/DelilahDevlin

Made in the USA
San Bernardino, CA
21 January 2017